What the Horned God Can Teach You

This is a book about balance — within the world and within oneself. The New Age cultus has become so obsessed with the Divine Feminine that they have neglected Her consort — the twin brother and lover — who balanced Her in all things and all ways. If the New Age is not to founder through lack of balance, this primal Horned God must be brought into our lives as purely as possible.

This book is for anyone who wants to learn about his or her inner heritage and at the same time transform himself or herself. It will help inform, expand, and direct the consciousness of the reader into areas of wonder and delight. Most of all, it will enable the reader to make direct, vital, and wholesome contact with his or her own most ancient potentials, as exemplified by the Horned God and Goddess.

Using the simplest of techniques, available to everyone in any circumstance, *Earth God Rising* shows how you can create your own Mystery and bring about real magical transformations without the need for groups, gurus, elaborate ceremonies, or expensive credit-card arrangements.

The impulse and energy of the Horned God is within each of us. It is both a separate reality and yet integral to the individual psyche. *Earth God Rising* shows us how to awaken and work with Him and bring ourselves into the New Age in a truly balanced manner.

About the Author

Alan Richardson was born in Northumberland, England, in 1951, and has been writing on the topic of magic for many years. He does not belong to any occult group or society, does not take pupils, and does not give lectures or any kind of initiation. He insists on holding down a full-time job in the real world like any other mortal. That, after all, is part and parcel of the real magical path. He is married with two children and lives very happily in a small village in the southwest of England.

To Write to the Author

We cannot guarantee that every letter written to the author can be answered, but all will be forwarded. Both the author and the publisher appreciate hearing from readers, learning of your enjoyment and benefit from this book. Llewellyn also publishes a bi-monthly news magazine with news and reviews of practical esoteric studies and articles helpful to the student, and some readers' questions and comments to the author may be answered through this magazine's columns if permission to do so is included in the original letter. The author sometimes participates in seminars and workshops, and dates and places are announced in *The Llewellyn New Times*. To write to the author, or to ask a question, write to:

Alan Richardson
c/o THE LLEWELLYN NEW TIMES
P.O. Box 64383-672, St. Paul, MN 55164-0383, U.S.A.
Please enclose a self–addressed, stamped envelope for reply, or $1.00 to cover costs.

LLEWELLYN'S MEN'S SPIRITUALITY SERIES

Earth God Rising

The Return of the Male Mysteries

Alan Richardson

1992
Llewellyn Publications
St. Paul, Minnesota, 55164-0383, U.S.A.

Cover painting by Peter Pracownik
Interior pencils by Blanca Apodaca

FIRST EDITION
Second Printing, 1992

Library of Congress Cataloging-in-Publication Data
Richardson, Alan, 1951-
    Earth God rising : the return of the male mysteries /
Alan Richardson
       p. cm.
    ISBN 0-87542-672-7
    1. Horned god. 2. Men — Religious life. 3. New Age
movement. I. Title
BL460.R53 1990
291.2'113—dc20   90-45552
                                                      CIP

Llewellyn Publications
A Division of Llewellyn Worldwide, Ltd.
P.O. Box 64383, St. Paul, MN 55164-0383

Llewellyn's Men's Spirituality Series

In recent times, the inevitable backlash to thousands of years of repressive patriarchy and de-valuation of the feminine has led to the re-emergence of women's spirituality and a new respect for the ancient Goddess. Yet now the balance seeks equilibrium — not a denial of men and everything male, but a new equality between the sexes.

Men may well and rightly revere the Goddess and seek to restore the lost feminine within themselves. Yet, in the process, they must not lose sight of the positive aspects of their own masculinity. There must be a male partner in the *hieros gamos*, the holy marriage within the psyche.

Llewellyn's Male Spirituality Series will explore these aspects and the possibilities that exist in today's world for male quests for the sacred and for the restoration of the awe and reverence due to our primordial male gods. Men must now forsake the negative and tyrannical aspects of the sexless gods of the patriarchies and embrace instead the wisdom of Odin, the compassion of Osiris, the justice of Zeus, and the moral strength of Krishna. Neither should we overlook the law-giving leadership of the god of Moses, the mercy and self-sacrifice of Jesus, the call to honor and righteousness made by Muhammad, nor the announcement of the New Aeon by Ra-Hoor-Khuit.

Today, in an age that is witnessing the return of the Goddess in all ways and on all levels, there is also a need to find, and *re-define,* the God within. Men—and women—need to know and to experience The Divine Masculine as well as The Divine Feminine so that the God, too, may be renewed.

Other Books by Alan Richardson

An Introduction to the Mystical Qabalah
Gate of Moon:
    Mythical & Magical Doorways to the Otherworld
Dancers to the Gods
Priestess: The Life and Magic of Dion Fortune
20th Century Magic

With Geoff Hughes:

Ancient Magicks for a New Age

To:

Angela Barker, for helping me find the Spring of the Green Man on outer and inner levels

Billie John and Laura Jennings for bringing me sparks from the Old Land

Peter Larkworthy for his timely appearance and insights

Kirsty Jane for her own particular kind of magic and wonder

And especially to Bobbie Gray for teaching me the best things, in ways that she will never have guessed.

Table of Contents

Introduction

This is a book about the Horned God. It is also a book about our innermost selves as they have extended back through the remotest past, from that past into our dire present, and toward our ultimate future.

At first thought, the Horned God exists somewhere between the designations of oddity and anachronism, and is invariably dismissed as little more than the crude focus of our even cruder ancestors. Today, in an age that is witnessing the return of the Goddess in all ways and on all levels, the idea of one more male deity may seem to be a step backward.

But the Horned God is, in fact, our oldest god. He was worshipped in light and love before humanity could even write words such as these. He was the true consort of that primal Goddess who is so fervently invoked as the intended cure for all our ills today. If and when this Goddess returns to inaugurate the New Age toward which we all aspire, she will not exist in isolation. She will want her man back with her. In fact, she is only returning because, at long last, she can sense the Horned God, who is also the Earth God, rising to meet her as he did in the old days of her happiness.

This whole book is based upon a premise found within the field of magic — an art for which I make no apology and one for which I offer very little in the way of interpretation. It is the premise that those world-problems caused by the negative aspects of male-dominated societies can be cured *not* solely by reaching toward the female aspects of divinity, but by invoking those forgotten and positive aspects of our most ancient god. The Horned God is just, never cruel; firm but never vindictive. The Horned God loves women as equals — one of the reasons why he was torn to pieces in the first place. He never could have imagined a world in which the feminine principle was not in perfect balance with the masculine. If the New Age is not to founder through a lack of such balance, and through a distortion of natural justice, then he must be invoked as clearly and as ardently as the Goddess who is his twin.

The story of the Horned God can be followed through from cave paintings in Stone Age France, along various and wondrous temples of ancient Egypt, glimpsed within the fabled hills of Camelot, and touched amid the forest depths of medieval Europe.

Can modern men and women find personal relevance in such a story today? They can if they want. In fact, we can all expect to find something of the Horned God's spirit within our genes. It is part of our psychological and spiritual heritage, our magical roots.

Can modern souls do anything practical about awakening the Horned God's qualities within themselves and within the world at large? They can if they want. Intention is half the battle. The final chapter of this book contains exercises to help the process.

The actual construction of this book is simple. The first chapter deals with the myth of Osiris, particularly in his earliest role as both Horned God and Green Man. His family origins and marital fate are subsequently used as a matrix against which we can measure and compare equally numinous myths from other Western sources. The Arthurian cultus is analyzed in order to enable us to look at the same energies in a more Celtic and Anglo-Saxon focus. Aspects of the Wild Hunt, the ancient stag cults and fertility religions, plus the time-lost worship of the Divine King are also analyzed in this Osirian light — not because I believe he was the first Horned God, but because he seems the best documented.

The primary purpose of the book is not to pass on a dry-as-dust occult history of debatable accuracy, but to awaken a sense of wonder, and to show that even the most obscure and esoteric symbols from the realm of near-forgotten myth can have immediate relevance to our modern lives. These myths, these "histories," represent energies and consciousness to be found tucked away at the back of our brains. Through them we may transform ourselves without the aid of gurus, without groups and their dogmas, without that modern process of enlightenment by credit card — and without surrendering our individualities.

The Horned God exists without and within. He represents a primal energy within the male and female that we scarcely have begun to acknowledge, much less to tap. The Horned God of the New Age does *not* want our worship — the time for that sort of thing is over. He wants to work with us as co-equals, for that is the only way forward. Call upon him and you can begin one of the most extraordinary journeys of your life.

Luck and good speed to you all.

— Alan Richardson
Wessex, England

The Journey Into Egypt

The magic of Egypt is older than the human mind can grasp. Dates and figures can be quoted but few people can really comprehend the spans of time involved. When the Dynastic Era began in 3150 B.C., there were deities and customs in existence whose origins were lost in the mists of time even then.

When we look toward the heart of Egypt from our cozy worlds at the brink of the 21st century, our first impressions are necessarily of bewilderment: gods and goddesses as numberless as the stars; each one having several aspects; each aspect changing over the centuries, often modified by religious fads or foreign invasions.

When we look into Egypt for the first time it is like looking into a child's kaleidoscope: millions of images, shifting and turning.

The only way to deal with it is to switch off the adult mind with its half-knowledge, its comparative and analytic tendencies, and take on the air of a little child who sits upon a strange and distant shore, looking out over a calm ocean with a clear mind.

That way the mysterious image known as Atum can arise and—ultimately—the whole spirit of Egypt with it. Begin with that immensely simple image, and that immensely simple frame of mind, and soon the kaleidoscope will transform itself into a telescope, through which we can glimpse another world ...

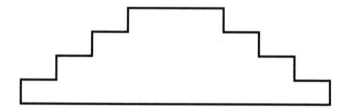

The Primeval Mound

It began, then, with Atum, "the Complete One," known also as the "Becoming One," who was visualized as the primeval hill, or mound—the first part of the land to appear from the depths of the waters, and the place where the High God dwelled as light. Sometimes, Atum was known by the rather splendid title of "Master of the Castle of Primeval Forms." Although the scribes tended to refer to Atum using the masculine grammatical gender, they all knew that Atum was really bisexual—"the great He-She" as one text put it. From the seed spilled by an act of self-applied sexual magic—that is to say, masturbation—there was born the brother and sister known as Shu and Tefnut. Really, being the only entity in the whole expanse of the infinitely empty universe, Atum had no choice but to mate with himself. And sometimes, in the desolation of our mortal lives, when we are surrounded by darkness and emptiness, it is only self-love in some form or another which can help lift us above the waters. We all know Atum.

Shu was the air and Tefnut the moisture, although the latter was sometimes also called Mayet, which means "world order." Mayet is more commonly known as Maat, crudely translated as "Truth." Her symbol is a feather, and she represents the balance between opposites: the ripening corn and the desert sand, the light and the dark, the inner and the outer. Maat whispers to us all the time; she is the feather-like touch of gnosis.

Nu and Geb

They produced in their turn the Goddess Nu, that

elegant woman of the sky who is pictured naked, and arched over the Earth, while beneath her is Geb, the Earth God, brother and lover, hard with desire and striving upward. He is seen kicking at the air to gain support, his member striving toward the stars and the ultimate union that he can see, smell, and anticipate until his heart almost bursts, but which he can never *quite* touch. Not in the daytime. Not in full consciousness. We know Geb only too well, we men do. We spend lifetimes with him, seeking a grip, striving hard. And Geb knows what all men secretly know everywhere, and invariably fight against: that Nu has the power, that hers is the strong position. Nu-woman (and new woman) comes down at *her* need, in the night, making dreams.

We can look at the Family Tree at this point, and try to remember.

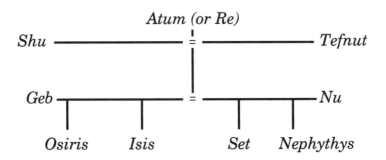

Family Tree of Egyptian Gods

It is the children we must focus on: the two males Osiris and Set, the two females Isis and Nephthys. It was from these four souls that the majesties and miseries of the world derived. (There was a fifth, but we need not be concerned with him yet.)

When Nu gave birth to Osiris at Thebes, a great voice was heard at the temple crying that the lord of all was entering into the light. His names were written with the symbols of a throne and an eye, which are tentatively transcribed as Ås-År or Us-Ar. He also had many symbols ascribed to his regency, such as the *djed* column, which referred to his resurrection, which we see as an image of the the crook and flail by which he guided or scourged as necessary, from which he gained the title of First Shepherd; the *atef* crown, which comprised the white crown of Upper Egypt and the two red feathers of Busiris plus, in many depictions, the solar disk and a pair of horns. Sometimes his body was colored red for the earth but more usually green for the vegetation. Osiris was the first Green Man. He was clearly identified with the constellation of Orion the Hunter, whom the Egyptians saw as a striding man forever looking behind him.

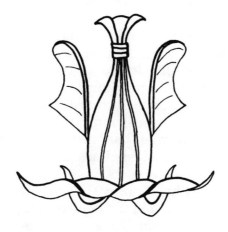

The Atef Crown
Osiris is immanent. He is the sufferer with all mortality but at the same time he is the power of

revival and fertility in the world. He is the power of
growth in plants and of reproduction in animals
and human beings. He is both dead and the source
of all living. To become one with Osiris is to become
one with the cosmic cycles of death and rebirth...[1]

He was the god of the common people, supreme
symbol of the life-force, "the force that through the
green fuse drives the flower." He is in fact Geb's heir,
and in this sense takes over the crown of the Earth God.
In early times, accordingly, he was worshipped in
"tombs" which consisted of a tumulus in the middle of a
grove. These mounds contained chambers which were
reached by winding passages. Here, in the Underworld,
the seeker could commune with Osiris.

The details intimidate at first. A strange god
worshipped at weird altars. And what woman has never
crawled into a lonely bed, sinking down into labyrinths
of despair, following the endless turnings of a ravaged
heart to try to reach that one, pure image within—to try
to reach man as he should be but never is: a man
wrapped like a gift and shiny-new, a present for the
woman alone, the first love and true love who, at the
core, can never fade, and must never decay. What
woman has never reached toward that Osirian spark
within her son, lover, husband, or father? The woman
hasn't been born who has never worshipped this
strange god at those weird altars. They search for him
constantly, in all of his parts.

Then there is his twin, with whom he fell in love
when still in Nu's womb, the beloved Isis. She became
perhaps the most enduring and dominant of all the
figures within the Egyptian pantheon, her worship
lasting for thousands of years and spreading throughout the Mediterranean world and beyond.

Osiris bearing the crook, flail, and uas wand

As his twin, Isis shares part of his name: As-t, more simply Ast, or even Aset, which means a throne or a seat. She taught Osiris the practice of agriculture, gave mankind the arts of medicine, instituted marriage in the world, taught women the domestic arts of corn-grinding, flax-spinning and weaving, and generally functioned as the Great Enchantress, mistress of all the magic under the Moon. In later versions of her image she can be seen with the child, the infant Horus: she wears on her head a disk set between the horns of a cow, and she was often identified with Hathor, who came later, and from elsewhere. This often happens to Great Goddesses: their single nature becomes like a crystal lens; shafted by the light of man's perception, it breaks up on the other side into a complete spectrum of goddesses. But her unified symbol in the heavens was unquestionably the star Sirius, which they knew as Sothis.

The appearance of this star marked the beginning of a new year and announced the advance of the Inundation of the Nile. We can find her, and hear all of Egypt's voice, in the cry of all tiny children at play: "Mummy's coming, Mummy's coming—quick! quick!" This is because the safe terror and the happy fear as she strides into their little games echoes exactly the voices along the Nile, when Sothis rose, bringing the waters.

Isis endures. That is her power. Through all the coming and going of men who become friends, lovers, husbands, and then become like little children again themselves—through all the bitter delights of having children who first adore, and then scorn and *then* love again, when they mature—she endures.

She holds things together as thrones can, when properly used. As a throne she bears weight, the kingly burdens of life. She is the one constant thing. As a throne, an empty throne, she is that which can take our weight, whose arms can offer us rest and protection. She wraps around us when we place the burdens of our bodies upon her, and in doing so we feel like kings and queens ourselves.

Isis is special, and makes us feel special. But she was chiefly worshipped for the part she played after the death of Osiris. Then she really came into her own.

Osiris was in fact murdered, which, in truth, is the only way for a god to die. Death by murder produces far more reverberations then the quiet decrepitude of age. The Osirian reverberations can still be felt. The culprit was his brother Set, who had always hated him. Set indeed believed that *he* should have been Geb's heir. And every time that Set looked upon his brother and saw how good, beautiful, perfect and beloved he was, he grew angry. We have all been in Set's place, too. We have all looked out through his mask. So it happened that Set invited Osiris to a banquet, a kind of "Last Supper" in which a gorgeous chest was brought out, and the offer made that whoever fit inside it perfectly could have it. The chest was illuminated with suns and stars, inlaid with precious jewels so that it looked like a model of the heavens themselves—not the anemic dots of light that we perceive above the neon polluted skys of our present world, but the staggering intensity of the ancient night when you could almost hear the music of the spheres and the sound of the wind through space, rushing between the worlds.

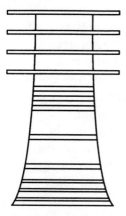

The djed column

Now Osiris was so good, so nice, that he loved and trusted his brother, and needed no second bidding to lie down within the chest, which fitted him perfectly. No sooner had he done so than Set and his 70 conspirators—like the animals they were—slammed the lid shut and nailed it down before casting it into the Nile. The English colloquialism, "he fitted me up," meaning that a person has been made a victim by cunningly arranged and carefully engineered circumstances, expresses this perfectly. Osiris was "fitted up."

Eventually, as the story goes, the coffin was washed ashore in Byblos, in Syria, where it became ensnared in the branches of a tamarisk tree, which in time enclosed the coffin completely within its own trunk. The tree in turn was cut down and taken to form a pillar in the palace of the King of Syria. This is one of the things represented by the *djed* column.

This is when Isis comes into her own, using her magic, her woman's knowledge, to follow the course of the coffin down the Nile before eventually tracing it into the palace. Disguised as an old woman acting as a nursemaid, her guise actually slips one night and the King of Syria, awed by her greatness, grants her the one wish important to her—to be given the pillar which contained the coffin of her beloved. Well, who could refuse Isis? Who could deny a goddess?

Triumphant, she returned home with the coffin and hid it on the isle of Chemmis, in the Delta. But as ill luck, woman's luck, would have it, Set and his 70 companions, while out hunting in the marshes, found the coffin and tore it open. They then ripped Osiris' body into 14 pieces which were then scattered over the length and breadth of Egypt. That, felt Set, was the only way to treat someone like Osiris. And Set was right, though for the worst of reasons.

Isis' search began in earnest then. She set out with her nephew Anubis (of whom more later) to find each piece. This is no problem for Anubis, the black dog or jackal who can sniff his way between the worlds. In some versions, whenever she found a piece she buried it with due honors—thus accounting for the many "burial places" of Osiris all over Egypt. In other versions she uses her magic to reassemble him. And what modern woman has never, even if only occasionally, craved the power to be able to do that to her husband—to reassemble him in the way that *she* wants? (However, it is usually left to the plastic surgeons to do this to wives, at their husband's request.) All agree that there was one piece of her husband's body—the phallus—which she did not find: It had been cast into the Nile and eaten by a fish, which Isis promptly cursed. Undeterred, she used her powers to create a replica either of gold or wood, which was every bit as potent as the real thing. From this, Horus was conceived. We will look more closely at him later, too.

Horus was raised by his mother and his aunt, Nephthys. He was taught how to fight, with all the berserker fury that only women can express, if they want. Despite being something of a cripple at birth—he was very weak from the waist down—he nevertheless grew strong, preparing himself daily until the time came when he would challenge his uncle for the Earth God's crown. In due course, after a mighty combat and much litigation in the courts of the gods, Horus triumphed.

And it is here that we find ourselves at a crucial juncture of our consciousness, for although Osiris could have reclaimed his throne, he preferred to maintain his kingdom in the Land of the Dead, and it was thus as God of the Dead that Osiris enjoyed his greatest popularity. Among other things, Osiris had learned that most difficult secret which many sons, lovers, husbands, and fathers never learn: when to hold, and when to let go. Osiris let go, and granted Horus the

Earth God's crown. He set Isis free in other ways, too.

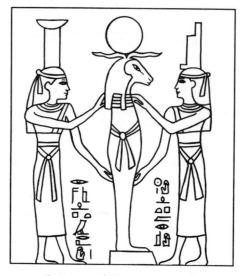

Osiris and Ra as one god,
sustained by Nephthys and Isis

Osiris' kingdom was supposed to be either beneath *Nun,* also called "Infinity, Nothingness, Nowhere, and Darkness," or in the Northern heavens, or else in the West. It is reminiscent of Western magical concepts of Atlantis. To the British mind this was in the West, and to the magicians of Germany to the North. The Kingdom of the Dead in the ancient world, however, was not some dread and dark place, but one of light and love. In a world of short lives and sudden death, it was the place where old loves could be renewed—not just for the fraught years of the mortal realm, but for the millions and millions of years of the Egyptian ideal. It was from the dead, who were usually buried in family and ancestral groupings at the edge of the desert (symbolic in itself) that a person's temporal power and wisdom was derived. It was Osiris who helped mediate these divine energies between the Underworld and this world. Every man in Egypt became an Osiris at death, not only for theological reasons but because it was as the First Love that he was always recalled, never in his ultimate geriatric form. And his *ka*, too, assumed that early vigorous shape of the deceased in his prime that souls will always assume in the immediate after-death states.

And that, in brief, is the story of Osiris. A story which continues today, ever-becoming. Nothing will ever change, or stop, until the world returns to Nun, to "Infinity, Nothing, Nowhere, and Darkness," as happens to all worlds eventually. But in our case it will happen sooner rather than later, unless we can learn to balance the gods within us.

These essential elements from the Osirian Cycle have been taken from the Heliopolitan version, which is the nearest thing to an "orthodoxy" that the whole of Egyptian Mythology possesses. Like any orthodoxy, and like the Bible, we can take images and quotations to support almost any proposition that we care to make. This, after all, is the whole purpose of myth. We stride through the apparent chaos of symbols and perform what magic we can to make those glyphs come alive which best respond to our own natures. In so doing, they can in turn make *us* come alive. By taking the bare bones of the Osirian myth, and assembling them to our own delight, we begin to assemble something wondrous within ourselves. The more we interpret and relate, the more we put veins and sinews and muscle-tissue upon the skeleton and find ourselves able to live life in a differing way, using new muscles of our own. All of it, no matter how trivial, how absurd, goes toward making

Osiris live again, and bringing life to ourselves.

Isis would like that.

Someone once said that only through children can we achieve immortality. While we might debate the truth of this statement, we can at least applaud the warmth behind it. Whoever said it, male or female, would certainly have loved Isis. No woman before or since has ever loved her husband, or her husband's children, as much as she did. As we have seen, her child by her brother Osiris was known as Horus. This is the Latinized form of the Egyptian Hor, or Heru. One of the earliest forms of Horus was Haroeris (or Harwer), derived from a combination of the Falcon God with the deity Wer, "the Great One," a serpent of light whose eyes were the Sun and Moon.

Isis awakes and knows that she is pregnant with the seed of her brother Osiris.

She rises, a woman in a hurry, her heart rejoicing . . .

To her mind Horus would, when born, become something of a wonder-child, a savior—not only for the world at large, but also for his father in the Underworld. Horus would bring light and love upon the earth, and the certainty of new beginnings. He would subdue those malicious forces represented by Set. Through him, in his falcon form, mankind would soar. This is the Great One, Wer, the serpent of light—but with wings—wings made from the feathers of Maat. This is the Earth God who has learned that formula whereby he can rise up toward the stars, instead of waiting for them to come down to him. It is a formula that derives from the serpent energies within the earth and within ourselves. This is the *kundalini* of Indian Tantrism. Horus, as his mother knew well, was and always will be the "sign of something coming." He is also Hope, that last creature within Pandora's Box, and the silver lining on every cloud. When things are bleak, Horus hawk-head is that which we can see hovering in the distance. As a child, brought up in secrecy on the floating island of Chemmis, in the marshes near Buto, he was known as Harpokrates, "the infant Horus." He was weakly and stunted from the waist down—perhaps because his father was dead when the child was conceived. During all his battles with Set to claim the Earth God's crown, the land itself suffered dreadfully. It became a wasteland. The crucial moment occurs when the triumphant son claims admission to his father's house in the Underworld, saying:

> Tell him that I have come hither to save
> myself and enliven my two cobras (eyes),
> to sit in the room of Father Osiris
>   and to dispel the sickness of the suffering god, so
>   that I
>   can appear an Osiris in strength,
> that I may be reborn with him in his renewed
>   vigour,
> that I may reveal to you the matter of Osiris' thigh
> and read to you from that sealed roll which lies
>   beneath his side,
> whereby the mouths of the gods are opened.[2]

Horus, as the King's heir and outer representative, is there to cure a mysterious wound in the thigh—a euphemism for the genitals—so that life will gush forth upon the land again. In order to cure Osiris fully, Horus first has to ask his father what ails him, in a manner that exactly parallels the question which had to be asked of the Fisher King in Arthurian mythology. The latter, ruler of a wasteland and keeper of the Holy Grail, suffered the same "wound in the thigh" as Osiris. In both cases, once the question is put, the wound heals, life gushes forth upon the land again, and Maat, order, is restored.

Perhaps Maat will make more sense if we think of her as representing the Balance of Nature, for this is closer to the meaning of Mayet/Maat than the concepts of Order, or Truth, that commonly have been used up until now. We will deal with the Holy Grail, and that mysterious "roll" concealed within Osiris' side in later chapters.

Isis with the child, Horus
(Porcelain statue in the Berlin Museum)

There is another secret concealed within the interchange of energies and consciousness between Horus and Osiris. It is simply that Osiris must *set himself* in motion and transcend his own helplessness. Horus can only do so much. The whole meeting between the victorious son and his paralyzed father is really an uncompromising exhortation to self-reliance. Once this attitude has been achieved within Osiris, and Horus has performed the mysterious ceremony known as the "Opening of the Mouth," using an adze which represents the constellation of the Great Bear (belonging to Set), the balance between the worlds *then* is truly restored, the inner and outer worlds fertile again. All of this can be restated in very simple terms:

We need Osiris. Osiris needs us.

We need the Land. The Land needs us.

Redemption has always been a two-way process, whatever the mystery.

Much of this is made more comprehensible in the light of Maat. She is, as already stated, the balance between the opposites: Upper and Lower Egypt; the fertile valley and the desert; good and evil, and so on. She was the very basis of civilization and the true source of Egypt's strength, and was perhaps the earliest attempt to express the concept of Nature—not simply in the sense of a green world teeming with life, but as a world existing and thriving through a divine and perfect order. Maat teaches us all we know about ecology and ergonomics, food chains, natural cycles, and all those patterns of life and death which influence us all. She was to be found within the Judgment Hall of Osiris, into which she ushered the soul of the deceased. She was then placed in one pan of the balance while the heart of the deceased was placed in the other. If the scales balanced, the heart was said to be "justified," and "true of voice." It thus fitted into its allotted place in the divine order—which was also the natural order of the world. Horus, then, put the world to rights by revivifying the inner kingdom of Osiris, and that outer kingdom which he now ruled himself.

Set, meanwhile, had been brought in chains before the gods. They only spared him on the condition that, as god of the wind and storms, he would convey the boat of Osiris through the Underworld. Well, he had little choice, really. Poor old Set—it was only through his imperfections that Osiris' faultless nature was given any meaning. How can we measure "goodness" unless we have a yardstick of "badness" to measure it by? It was Set who made the gods god-like. As the worst among us, he should be given the best of our love; but that is an arcanum that humanity is not yet ready or willing to achieve.

The goddess Maat

His heritage now restored, Horus was declared ruler of the two Egypts, and titled *Har-pa-Neb-Taui*, "Horus, Lord of the Two Lands." This was a title later echoed by the pharaohs themselves, who all took the name Horus as one of their own. This reminds us of the practice of always giving male heirs to the throne of the British

Royal Family the name of Arthur somewhere in their long list of first names. Then began the long but happy process of rebuilding all those temples of his ancestors which Set had destroyed. Then began another Age within the world.

We who stand here on the polluted shores of the Piscean Age, watching the waters ebbing away with the final years of this century, can see the fishes themselves giving their last gasps in the strange atmospheres that are now being revealed to them. We can, with some delight and awe, and no little fear, watch Horus swoop down upon the last years of this era to pluck up one of those fishes within his talons. The death of the Piscean Age is hastened as he feeds upon it and builds up his own strength, absorbing the creature's power as an Aztec warrior would consume his enemy's heart. The fish itself contains the debris of our own wearied civilizations. But it also contains that long lost phallus of Osiris. And to help us leave the realms of simple myth and enter those of magical prophecy even further, we must now consider the nature of that other son: We must now consider Anubis.

To understand the son, however, we must first look at his mother. Gods are no different from us in this respect. Nephthys was Nu's second daughter, and although she was married to Set, her love and passion was for Osiris. As wife to the wretched god of aridity and tempest, she conceived no children to make her own life happier, and so in despair she disguised herself as her sister, Isis, in order to sleep with her true love. The result of this union was Anubis. (The more purely Egyptian form of the name is Anpu.) If Isis is the wo- man who endures, Nephthys is the one who *survives*. We see her in the single parent who will bring up her child or children despite all the odds, and who has still got something left over for herself. We see her in the sort of woman who has the chameleon powers to blend into any background, for any purpose, or else who becomes an active shape-shifter—able to become, on the surface, what people want her to be, while retaining an inner spark that is unique and unquenchable. Isis *is*, to make a word-play, but Nephthys constantly mirrors change,

Her son, Anpu, was a fine son, the sort any goddess would be proud to have. Seeing him as a dog or jackal-deity, the Egyptians naturally associated him with the western desert, or the home of the dead. In some early sources he took over the title of the funerary god Khenti-Amentiu, "First of the Westerners." Another of his titles, in his full jackal form *Wepwawet,* was "Opener of the Way." This is the title we must eventually fasten upon.

Anpu had a humor as black as his skin, though not without compassion, and an insight as bleak as the desert he haunted, though it was not without luminosity. He had—and has—all the power and blackness of a person who has long since mastered all the self-destructive urges within him and can now see the possibilities of mastering his own fate. As alert as his sharp ears indicate, he can hear things coming from hundreds of miles and thousands of years away. His memory, activated by his extraordinary sense of smell, reaches the full circle of forgotten past and unimagined future. Capable of cruelty, he yet became the Guardian of women and small children. He is his mother's son all right, but with a touch of Set in him somewhere.

Fearing Set's vengeance when he found out about her perfidy, Nephthys exposed her infant as soon as he was born, casting him adrift into the marshes—an act which she regretted instantly and so intensely that she fled and confessed everything to Isis. Her sister was then able to find the baby Anubis during her own searches for her husband. She adopted him and loved him as her own. This sounds as if it might be a casual enough piece of the story, or a mere linkage between the major episodes. But there is more to it than that. As we will see later, everyone who searches for Osiris, and what he represents, stumbles upon Anubis first.

Anubis—Opener of the Way

After this supreme act of sisterly love and intense jealousy on Isis' part, Nephthys joined her in all her trials. Together they found the body of Osiris. As kites, great long-winged birds of the falcon family, they mourned over his corpse. At times we can still hear them: the two voices within a woman at the breakdown of a marriage which say: *I'm going to take this from him, take everything, so that he won't leave me*—that is the thin voice of the diminutive Isis; and then: *I'll give the bastard hell, that way he won't do it again*—that is Nephthys in her rage.

These are not the goddess voices in full power, but instead voices heard distantly, down a long, long tube.

In early times Anubis was something of a Death God for the pharaoh alone—a sacred executioner, a Priest of Anubis, who would ritually murder the pharaoh by means of a viper at the end of a stipulated time. Some sources say 28 years.

Of all the other images discussed so far, remember that one. We will come back to it in some detail in later chapters.

In his role as Lord of Magic, Anubis could see the past and future with ridiculous ease. In fact he *was* the past and future, for he also came to be described as Time. In the role of Time, the Devourer, he is described as devouring the Apis Bull, one of the major symbols of Osiris himself, who was often known as *Kai Imentet*, the "Bull of the West."

Actual representations tend to show Anubis as a jackal-headed man, although this has sometimes been interpreted as a dog; whence the dog-headed Hermes in that mythology which the Greeks borrowed from Egypt. Sometimes he is shown accompanying Isis—an allusion to his role and title as Guardian. Small statuettes of him were kept by Egyptian bedsides, to guard over people's dreams, while even today magicians have been known to invoke his image and use it to protect properties, or else set him and his astral hounds loose beyond the peripheries of those circles within which they perform their Work. His symbol was a black and white ox-hide spattered with blood and hanging from a pole. And if we look closely at the large and upward-pointing ears, we will see that we are not *that* far from the Horned God who is central to our thesis.

Anubis was regarded as being identical to Osiris himself in many sources. At some centers, such as Oxyrhynchus and Cynopolis, the two were identical. It was E. A. Wallis Budge, the legendary Egyptologist and translator of the *Book of the Dead,* who speculated that the cult of Anubis was perhaps the most ancient of all, and that in some ways the Osirian Cult actually was consumed by that of the jackal. He wrote:

> Others again are of the opinion that by Anubis is meant Time, and that his denomination of *Kuon* [the Greek word for "dog"] does not so much allude to any likeness, which he has to the dog ... as to that other signification of the term taken from *breeding*; because Time begets all things out of it self, bearing them within itself, as it were in a womb.[3]

We can also associate him with the number 9. Multiply any number by 9, e.g. 9 x 13 = 117. Add the digits of the answer—1 + 1 + 7—and you get 9 again. This is Anubis doing in the world of Number what he does within our genes.

Apart from his relationship to, and identification with, Osiris, the god Anubis also functions as the Dark Twin in tandem with Horus as the Bright Twin. Even though these are roles taken from the mythological structures of megalithic Europe, they are still valid in this context. Anubis, who was conceived while Osiris was still "in the flesh," finds himself a creature of the Earth, linked with the natural cycles as Time itself.

Horus, who was conceived *after* his father's death, is more a creature of Fire and Air, swooping down from heights. And although it was the Hawk who inherited the kingship from Osiris, it will be Anubis, the Dark Twin and Sacrificial Priest, who will bring this kingship to an end, spill blood upon the land, and give life to the world anew.

That might not be clear yet, but it will be.

Here is a prophecy to go with it:

Soon, a woman will conceive by inseminating herself with the frozen sperm of her dead husband. The child, a boy, will have something wrong with his legs at first. But after intense treatment, paid for by his aunt, he will become almost as mobile as any child, except for a slight limp he will have for all of his short life. The boy, inheriting his father's talents, will set the world and the hearts of women alight . . .

This, so far, has been a fairly exoteric introduction to the standard myths relating to the particular figures. The purist might quibble that no reference has been made to other versions of this mythology, or to major figures such as Horus the Elder, Thoth, Ptah, Sekhmet, or the enigmatic and important *Benu* Bird, who is seen at the Beginning and the End of Time. Indeed the list of omissions is endless, the areas of overlap and interaction almost infinite. Still, no apology can, should, or will be made; persons must find their own myths and work them through. That is what they are for. They are to initiate people. In the strictest sense of the word, myths are there to help them "begin." This *beginning* is everything—far more important than purity or accuracy of scholarship, far more vital than a correct assembly of all the scholarly facts. As soon as people begin to work with their myths—however crudely—the myths begin to work with them. They become Initiates from then on.

So we must now strike an attitude and play a game. There is no need to go back over the earlier details to try to fully remember and comprehend everything—at least not yet. The vital work is already being done by the subconscious, in that sort of subliminal brooding which will eventually produce surface results.

First, we must adopt that childlike but not childish attitude in which we can approach the Heliopolitan Recension with all the wonder, awe, and delight that we once reserved for our favorite fairy-tales. In doing this, we must realize that each part is vital to the whole, and resist the adult temptation to isolate and analyze and invariably venerate. Who cares, when they are three years old, what Snow White can symbolize? Or that great sociological commentaries can be found within the names of the dwarfs ... The important thing is what they did, and how. Similarly Isis cannot be considered without her consort, nor Anpu without his mother. This is not sexism, but balance, for the gods are all part of us, and the parts must function properly.

That is the attitude—a deliberate attempt not to be clever. The game we must play is also a simple one. It is really the direct opposite of the attitude, and uses the other side of the brain. Basically, we must try to relate the functions of the gods (as we understand them) to mundane items of daily life.

Take a flashlight for example. Osiris is the battery, Horus is the bulb, Nephthys the switch, Anubis those fittings which conduct the circuit of electricity, Isis the case which contains them all—and Set the darkness which creates the flashlight's very purpose.

Or: Osiris is the seed, Isis the soil, Horus the sun which brings the growth.

Or: Osiris is the gasoline, Isis the ignition chamber,

Horus the ignition spark—and Set the exhaust gases.

Or: Anything, really. It is a game that you can only win, there can be no losers. In a very real sense it begins to awaken to the gods within the world, and therefore within the magician's own consciousness.

The game and the attitude are both opposites, and both must be developed. Switch on, switch off, right and then left... In time the Opener of the Way himself will come to help.

Set

There is one final concept that we must consider before continuing. It is the nature of that Underworld in which Osiris chose to remain, known to the Egyptians as *Dat, Duat,* or even *Tuat,* pronounced exactly like the English vulgarism "twat." Although this concept has been ignored or minimized, it actually provides each magical tradition with its real sources of power and endurance.

To the Egyptians, death and life were just different sides of the same door—aspects along the same polarity. This polarity could be seen at every level—animal, vegetable and mineral. One was nothing, meaningless, without the other. The Underworld was where things were given the shape and form in which they would later appear within this world. It is the astral plane, and the subconscious mind. Despite the convenient term "Underworld," the *Tuat* was in fact given no specific location. Most often it was regarded as being under the Earth, but it was sometimes regarded as being beyond the vault of the stars—or else in those waters that they imagined extended everywhere beneath the land. The symbol for the Underworld was

⊗ , while the symbol for the stars was ✳ .

Not a great deal of difference there. "It is the place of the formation of the living out of the dead and the past, the true meeting-place of time before and after." Its gates were protected by fire-spitting serpents, lions, or dragons, and by a sphinx-like creature known as the Aker, which held the eastern and western portals. It is therefore the place of the ancestors, of souls long dead and yet waiting to be born. In some senses it is the cerebellum, containing all our racial memories, and in others it is the womb. The symbol ⊗ , which so temptingly asks to be transformed into the ☆

beloved of modern occultists, should perhaps be regarded more like a sphincter which is capable of being pushed, peeled, or pried open, thus:

Through that narrow entrance is the Underworld. It is the opened cervix leading to the womb. The *Tuat,* and the twat, is the means by which we can give birth to ourselves.

Notes

[1]R. T. Rundle Clark, *Myth and Symbol in Ancient Egypt.* (London: Thames and Hudson, 1959), p. 97.

[2]*Ibid.,* Coffin Text No. 228.

[3]E. A. Wallis Budge, *The Gods of the Egyptians.* (London: Routledge and Kegan Paul, 1904), Vol. II, pp. 264-265.

Budge was long rumored to have been linked with a magical group which met in the basement of the British Museum, using the Egyptian artifacts there as the basis for their temple.

And Then Camelot

All myths are in fact living energies. We have decided that much. The ones in question were ancient when the First Dynasty began around 3100 B.C. — and yet they are no age at all. They are instead ever-becoming, like the spurting of Atum, or the column of some sparkling and infinite fountain. How to find that fountain, and when to drink from it, is something that we can spend a lifetime studying only to find (as seekers always do) that it is within us all along.

One of those figures from the realms of myth and history who was more aware of such matters than most was a certain priest from the 26th Dynasty. Now *he* knew all about this sort of thing, as he never ceased to tell anyone who cared to listen. Many of the people thought him insufferable because of this, but the man had absolute conviction as to his merit and his destiny, and he never ceased to prophesy. That was what he was best at.

His name was Ankh-f-n-Khonsu, which means "His heart is with Khonsu." Khonsu was the old Moon God from Thebes, where the mysteries functioned on a more subconscious level than elsewhere. This Dynasty, which ran from 663 to 525 B.C. — as near as such things can be determined — saw pharaohs bearing the names Necho and Psamtik and Ahmose supporting their rule by Osirian doctrines rather than through the purely solar cults which had taken over in previous centuries. Set — it was always Set — became the personification of darkness again; the great arts and styles of the Old Kingdom were recreated; a colossal granite temple for the Apis Bull was built at Saqqara; and the Egyptians were able to imagine for a little while that true greatness had been restored to their land. Ankh-f-n-Khonsu, who lived a full life sometime during those reigns, was the priest who brought about the Aeon of Osiris to replace that of Isis. And, as is the way of magic, he was also the one who brought it to an end.

If Ankh-f-n-Khonsu died in the 26th Dynasty, then at the same time, through one of those tricks understood only by Anubis, he was reborn in 1875, not far from an old tree in Leamington Spa, Warwickshire, which was widely held to be at the exact center of England. This was also a time historians would come to regard as being the absolute zenith of the British Empire. Later on, his life would continue to echo this local belief in the way that he saw himself as the Omphalos, the divine navel or center — not merely of England, to which he had an ambivalent attitude, or of the Empire, which was the greatest ever seen — but of the entire world — and perhaps substantial portions of the universe too. His mother, a prim lady of the narrowest kind, was never to understand all this. There was not much of the compassionate Isis in *her*. She was never able to see her son as Ankh-f-n-Khonsu, Prince Chioa Khan, Frater Perdurabo, or as any of the many other masks and names he assumed in his extraordinary life. To her, he was simply Edward Alexander Crowley, her difficult son; and if he was to call himself also, more enduringly, Aleister, and claim to be bringing to the world visions from beyond Time, then that was something she did not want to know about at *all*.

Crowley in fact holds many of the threads that will form the warp and woof of this narrative, and in due course we will be able to see how these can be pulled together though him to form a garment of pure light. He was, along with his one-time mentor Samuel Liddell "MacGregor" Mathers, one of those magicians who actively worked at bringing the Egyptian Mysteries out into the consciousness of the West. Mathers was the greater magician, but Crowley had one inestimable advantage: his was one of he most marvelously dreadful, warped, and unforgettable personalities of all time. Yet he used this personality like a crystal boat — a dream-craft able to carry dead (or as yet unawakened) souls with him.

But did he, and many others like him, actually bring the Great Gods of Egypt into the Western consciousness, or where they here already?

Many occultists have argued that the Egyptian mysteries gradually, over vast periods of time, spread westward. Either via migrating peoples, or traders, taking their gods with them in much the same way that Asian shopkeepers in Britain today have brought Islam, Buddhism, and Hinduism with them. Or else they were brought by conquest, via the Greeks and Romans who had long been heavily influenced by the cults of Isis and Osiris in some form. In her elegant book, *Awakening Osiris,* Normandi Ellis lists some of the words in the modern English language that she feels to be of Egyptian origin:

arm — *armen*
hex — *heku*
nebulous — *neb*
satisf — Satis (goddess of the flood, or meaning
          "enough")
aura — *aor* (magic light)

These words would probably not convince the etymologist, but, because the author approaches the topic with the eye of a poet (and a very sensual one at that), we can cheerfully accept them at one level of truth if at no other. Nevertheless, if all Western languages can be traced back to an Indo-European original, then we are a step closer to acknowledging that Egyptian influences of more than one sort did indeed spread westward. In a similar vein, J. P. Cohane, who *was* an etymologist, concluded that "in ancient times, before the Carthaginians, the Egyptians, the Greeks, and the Romans, certain key names and words were taken out in all directions from the Mediterranean [and have survived] in spite of corruptions, in the names of rivers, mountains, volcanoes and waterfalls, lakes and islands, regions, towns and cities, scattered all across the face of the earth."[3] He may well be a little over-enthusiastic here, but with such a vast theme it is never any good trying to subtly understate the case. We could, however, take his words and jiggle them about a little: "In ancient times, certain key names, and words, and religious concepts were taken out in all directions from the Mediterranean. . . ." That would be better, perhaps. It might even be true. And it would also explain why Osirian imagery can be found to underlie some of the more numinous aspects of what has become known as the Western Mystery Tradition.

It has also been argued, and sometimes effectively, that the more spectacular examples of megalithic culture in Britain — notably Stonehenge and Avebury — were the creation of Egyptian priest-scientists. Archaeologists and anthropologists were once adamant that similarities between the chambered tombs of Britain and the *mastabas* built in Egypt in the 3rd millennium B.C. were too close to be altogether accidental.

Were Aleister Crowley and MacGregor Mathers and all the other magicians in Britain and the West merely responding to a fad in adopting the gods and goddesses of Egypt as their primary inspirations? Or were they really touching upon the exotic origins of their own nation's most ancient mysteries? It would be a simple enough debate if it wasn't for Atlantis.

Many magicians insist, usually on the basis of their own inner visions, that the true origins of their esoteric heritage can be found in the West, in that sunken land below the Atlantic Ocean. Before Atlantis went down, they insist further, active units of priests and priestesses were sent off in all directions. Some of them made it to Britain and western Europe, others to Egypt, either directly by sea, or via various overland routes through Africa. Still others headed westward and thus helped found the Mayan cultures or even — much further north — influenced the North American Indian. Everything stems from that lost continent, they say. By this, they explain the fundamental similarities between the mythologies and magics of different nations.

If we can resist its seductive appeal for a moment, can we *really* believe in Atlantis? We can if we want. There will always be enough convincing evidence to support the believers, and never quite enough to sway the skeptics.

The *sense* of Atlantis, however, is unmistakably a sense of great age but incomparable vigor; a peculiar sort of pride — such as a Harvard man might feel next to a graduate from some hillbilly institute; and the feeling, indeed the knowledge, that there are sources of real but eldritch power available for you when needed.

The most enduring image from all the Atlantean mythology cf the modern magicians, however, is that of the three-tiered mountain rising from the waters, on top of which lived the priest-kings, the Atlantean elite, the focus of whose lives revolved around the temples dedicated to working with the solar, lunar, and stellar forces. These were the people, it was felt, who influenced the evolution of the entire world.

We must focus on the mountain, however, rather than the accretions to it. Wipe out the inhabitants, and we are left with Atum's mound above the waters, later echoed by those "Mounds of Osiris" left behind whenever the water of the Nile had withdrawn. We are left with such bare and pure equivalents as Glastonbury Tor, which is the focus of many Avalonian Mysteries, or with Ayers Rock in Australia, Mt. Kailas, Mt. Shasta — and indeed every emanating power-source which has ever been heaved up beyond the sea level and into human awareness.

We experience Atlantis in our own ways, if we want, but we can best deal with it for the moment by regarding it as an Essence, to apply a medieval term. Charles Fielding, a modern magician of formidable experience asserts that it is not simply a place, but an entire set of conditions that probably went on for at least ten thousand years. "It was a whole *series* of civilizations — in both an area and a period of time."[4]

To describe something as Atlantean is akin to all those American advertisements which evoke the term "European" to give their product a particular tone, a certain quality. We can believe, if we want, but for the rest of this book let us accept it as an essence, just as Hollywood is an essence: a place whose true impact and reality is to be found more within the hearts and minds of its admirers than within the concrete of its streets.

Of course, peoples of every nation tend to regard their own lands as being peculiarly sacred, home of the gods, and host to whatever Second Coming is most appropriate. Being an Englishman first and a Briton second, I am no different.

> To the peoples of antiquity the isle of Britain was the very home and environment of mystery, a sacred territory, to enter which was to encroach upon a region of enchantment, the dwelling of the gods, the shrine and habitation of a cult of peculiar sanctity and mystical power. Britain was, indeed, the *insula sacra* of the West, an island veiled and esoteric, the Egypt of the Occident.

This is quoted from *The Mysteries of Britain,* by Lewis Spence, a Scot who had been a member of *An Uileach Druidh Braithreachas* or the Druid Universal Bond[5] and one of those rare types who was able to combine a passion for magic with a genuine scholar's learning, delivered in a wondrously fluent style. Spence may have been writing, with no small pride, about his native land, but his opinions would have been shared completely by Julius Caesar, who came, saw, and finally conquered much of Britain in 55 and 54 B.C. To Caesar's mind, the Druid religion began in that country and found its highest expression there.

Unfortunately, the Druids too have become something of an *essence,* invariably visualized as cerebral, clean, restrained, and philosophical fellows with white robes and stern miens — rather like castrated versions of the average English Bishop today. But the reality was far different, far more virile, infinitely more "savage," and more akin in style to the shamans of the American Indians than anyone else.

This is one of the reasons why reputable pre- and post-War psychics in Britain were bewildered to "see" what they assumed to be Indian or even Mayan communities at the megalithic sites, causing them to speculate on various migratory theories and occult histories. Yet in truth they were seeing native British life in the raw, without the usual Victorian projections.

Britain was known on the continent as the Isle of the Dead, the westernmost world beyond the ocean where young priests were sent to further their training in the Mystery Colleges on Salisbury Plain — an area where Britain now maintains its top-secret aeronautical research establishments, germ warfare laboratories, and a host of military encampments. Even today, the Plain, when night is falling, is not a *nice* place to be. And much later, in the nearby levels of Somerset, the Druidic practices gave way to those traditions which had sprung up about Joseph of Arimathea having founded the first Christian Church in Glastonbury, followed by the mystical King Arthur and all those traditions about the Holy Grail which gave the Arthurian Cycle its energy. Britain was then (and still is, if you know where to look) a world of stone circles and sacred springs, mysterious tombs and remnant temples, legends and ley lines and colossal earth Zodiacs built into the terrain, of witches, dragons, gods and ghosts — especially ghosts. Britain, the British proudly claim, is the most haunted country in the world.

Now it was once the fashion to describe magic in terms of "rays": there was the Egyptian Ray, the Celtic Ray — invariably but misleadingly associated with the Green Ray, a Norse Ray, Christian Ray, and so on. A more useful if cruder analogy, however, can be lifted from the science of geology. Egyptian magic, far from being a ray of light, is more akin to one of those tectonic plates which support whole continents, and which constantly "drift" across the globe. It is the collision with the tectonic plate of Indian mysticism that has caused tremors, massive surging energies, and disruptions which have raised mountains and nations. It is within these disruptions and break-aways upon the earth's surface that we can find the smaller, but by no means "inferior," mysteries of the West which found expression among the Germanics and/or Teutons and the rest — all of which overlapped in one way or another.

As we have noted, it is a generally accepted theory about the population of Western Europe that a succession of peoples moved westwards from some point of origin in Asia Minor — the traditional Garden of Eden. These migrations were like ripples in a pool, each successive ripple of humanity driving the previous incumbents on westward until there was only Britain and Ireland before them. If nothing else, Britain, particularly, became something of a melting pot, and most of the pantheons of Europe and beyond found expressions there in some form at some time. Nowadays, thanks to individuals and organizations like the Wright Brothers and the Cunard Line, the same thing is happening within America, with the same ultimate result,

So if there is an Egyptian stratum of consciousness, there is also what might be termed the Avalonian stratum lying somewhere above it. By Avalon is meant a realm which, although linked inseparably to real places, is not entirely within this world. Britain might be the body, but Avalon is the *ka,* or spirit, in the eyes of many. Egypt had its masculine focus in Osiris, who was the Green Man, Corn King, and Horned God: Avalon, in contrast, had King Arthur.

If the Druids have been given the Hollywood treatment (and there is a small joke buried there which would cause any decent Druid to smile), then the same can be said about Arthur — perhaps more so. The image we retain of him is more akin to Richard Coeur de Lion, the Black Prince, or the mythical Saint George than anyone else. If Arthur existed at all, then he would have been a dark-haired Celt, someone who fought on foot, and with little of the chivalric manners invested in him by those medieval romancers who came a thousand years after his probable time. He *may* have historical origins as a Romano-British warlord who held off the Saxons for a brief spell. He may even have been a Breton warlord Arzur who did similar deeds, but his true role for our present purposes is to be found as the Once and Future King — the British Christ in some ways. Like all Sacred Kings, many places within many nations claim him for their own; or, as with Jesus, preserve myths which seek to "prove" that he once, and right fondly, visited their country.

Arthur is the son of Uther Pendragon. The origin of his name is not clear, although it is invariably linked with artos, "the bear." But can we, by listening very carefully to the sheer sound of these names Arthur and Uther, detect a resemblance to the names As-Ar and Us-er? We can if we want. The word for "mother," for example, has retained its shape and sound ever since its spread from the Indo-European original: Sanskrit - *matr;* Latin - *mater;* Old Irish - *mathir;* Old High German - *muotar;* Old Saxon - *modar;* Old English - *modor;* Old Frisian - *modor;* and Dutch *moeder.*

And here we must distinguish the formal "mother"

from the instinctive labial plosives used by babies when they call for "mum," "mom," or "mummy." These all become a *little* more plausible when we note the magical tradition which insists that Arthur was not the name of an individual but *an initiatic title.* Just as the pharaohs linked with Osiris in their names and titles, so might the name Arthur have been passed down through the kingships as a symbol of role, or function.

Yet before we can go further into this topic, we must first pause and take a simplified look at the main details of the Arthurian Cycle. It is not quite as simple a task as dealing with the Egyptian myths, because the latter used pictures — hieroglyphs to create words and concepts within the mind. The glyphs of the Egyptian pantheons are easy to hang onto, but in the Matter of Britain, as it is called, words are used to evoke pictures. It is a question of two separate cultures using different sides of the brain. This means we must visualize the Arthurian figures as best we can, seeing them with faces that are already known to us. And before we can do this with any of the better-known figures within the Cycle, we must begin at the beginning. We must look at Uther Pendragon.

Uther is possibly the most darkling of all the characters within the Arthurian Mysteries — although "character" is perhaps a misleading term when so little is known of his personal qualities. The phonetic similarity between he names of Arthur and Uther is so obvious as to be almost ignored, yet it helps give a little more substance to the concept of this being an initiatic title. This in itself is given a further boost by the name Pendragon. *Pen* is from the Cornish for "Head." So Uther, as *Head of the Dragon,* or even Dragon King, takes on a special significance when we consider the esoteric concept of the dragon or serpent as a symbol of the Earth's energies, and also as the terrestrial shadow of the Hawk.

Uther Pendragon fell in love with Ygraine, wife to Gorlois of Cornwall, but the love was not mutual. In fact, his suit was so futile that he was only able to press it further by means of magic. With the aid of Merlin the Enchanter, who enabled him to change shape for one night, he was able to impersonate Gorlois and attain "the pleasure of Ygraine's thighs," as it was once delicately put. As with all magical matings, a child was conceived that same night and born in due course. This of course was Arthur.

Under an arrangement with Ygraine, who soon realized what had happened, Merlin took the child away and fostered him out to the kindly Sir Ector, of the Forest Sauvage, to raise him as his own. In the interim, Uther made himself High King. He died years later but left no apparent heir. After his death, a miraculous sword was seen plunged irretrievably into an anvil mounted on a stone. This too, it turned out, was a feat which had been engineered by Merlin. The legend on the sword (which was *not* Excalibur) stated that whoever could pull the sword from the stone would be the rightful King of Britain.

Only the boy, Arthur, the Miraculous Child, was able to draw the sword from the anvil — to his own astonishment. It was then that Sir Ector revealed Arthur's true origins. Gradually the lesser kings accepted him. In due course, Merlin appeared once more to lead him toward a mystic lake wherein the arm of a Lady "clothed in white samite" rose from the depths of the lake bearing the sword Excalibur and its marvelous scabbard.

We might pause at this natural juncture and look at this a little more closely.

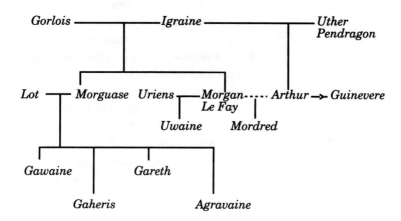

Arthur's Family Tree

It was the magician Violet Firth, who wrote under the pen-name "Dion Fortune," who hinted that the story of Ygraine, Uther, and Gorlois was in fact a shadowy version of cross-fertilization between a royal woman of Atlantean stock and one of the native Britons. The child would necessarily be "of the Blood," as she thought of it — a prince of the Sacred Clan which had once ruled Atlantis. This concept of the Blood Royal, or the *Sang-Real,* has persisted in various lines of mystical theory and magical practice down through to the present day. Dion Fortune was inclined to believe that she had been an Atlantean priestess herself in a previous life. She had certainly spent *many* other lives working in temples along the Nile.[6]

That is one of the interpretations. Another, not necessarily contradictory, approach might be that Uther was not so much a physical person but in fact a Kingly spirit on the inner planes, and one who overshadowed Gorlois so completely that one of the

love-makings with his wife became transformed into
something more than that, opening Gates between the
worlds and the womb which would allow a Son or
Daughter of Light to incarnate. This happens. It can
happen to one or both partners when it is necessary for
a soul of a particular type and destiny to be born. Sons
and Daughters of Light do not always function in
philosophical or religious areas of life. They are not
always apparent to the masses. Sometimes they can
seem to be dangerous characters indeed. And sometimes, when they just fail to express their Light in the
proper manner, they really can be become dangerous,
even if they are sparked with something sublime.

The fact that Merlin was involved points to the idea
that this was not merely an act of magically arranged
rape, but the sort of ritually charged sexual magic that
was well-known and perhaps fundamental to Mystery
Centers throughout the Classical world.

Whichever interpretation we choose, we are still left
with the concept of a sexual act linked with magical
practices that result in a child touched with divinity.
But despite the specious similarities which can be
drawn between Uther/Us-er and Arthur/Ås-År, we are
not *yet* firmly within the realms of Osirian parallels.
These begin to manifest more clearly in Arthur's adult
life, as will be shown. So far, all we need is to
acknowledge that Arthur and Osiris were both kings —
and indeed both Divine Kings; that they were linked
with the concept of illuminated rulership; and that
their names became used as initiatic titles for those
who followed.

Can we, however, find any clear Osirian parallels
which link that god with the image of the dragon, or
winged serpent, and thus show that the name Pendragon, too, really may have been more than just a

family name? Yes, we can. In *The Book of Caverns* we can see a very clear image of Osiris, deep in the Earth, enfolded by a serpent. This is *Wer,* "Most Ancient One," or Nehaher, "Fearful Face," or Mehen, "Encircler." To Egyptians, all the serpents or dragons were one, all linked with the Underworld, and both protective and retarding as all Earth energies can be. For Osiris to "rise up," the serpent had to be controlled, the telluric energies harnessed. In light of this, we can regard Arthur as one who "pens" or controls the dragon, thereby taking Pendragon in its English rather than Cornish interpretation. And, of course, the *uraeus,* the serpent symbol on the brow, came to be considered a supreme emblem of all the pharaohs' power. But what of Merlin? Although magicians, drawing on their qabalahs, have invariably associated him with the Ibis-headed figure of Thoth, he will soon show himself to be far more akin to Anubis. In an age when it is customary to analyze every goddess figure as something of a Triple Goddess (Maiden/Mother/Crone), we often forget that gods, too, can split themselves. Hermes, Thoth, and Anubis can in fact be seen as differing aspects of the one entity, being at once revealer and scribe of that which is revealed, at once Chthonian and Olympian, at once Gold and Black, above and below . . . this is the god who travels between the realms of humanity and divinity, linking one to the other. Merlin himself does exactly this, and contains within himself both the Horned God and the Black Dog.

In fact the Arthurian Cycle would surely fall apart without Merlin. He weaves himself in and out of it; he appears at crucial moments and indeed instigates these moments. In this respect he is like time itself, and also fate, for he brings into being certain incidents which hurry the cycle along to its terrible end. He is also, in his

Anubic role as a symbol of "breeding," clearly shown as responsible for the continuation of the Pendragon bloodline.

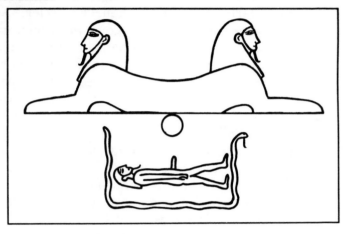

Osiris in the Underworld enfolded by
the serpent and guarded by Aker

There is no doubt that Merlin is more than a mere magician: he is the High Priest; he is the tester and confirmer of Kings — and Divine Kings at that. It was he who created the sword in the stone through which Arthur proved who and what he was.

Now, to the mind of the Ancient Britons, the sword was, *par excellence,* the weapon of choice for the royal and rich. A prestige weapon. Anyone could make a spear, but a sword could only be made through the most sophisticated technologies of the time, making use of the raw materials to be found within the Earth. Arthur's pulling the sword out of the anvil, which itself was placed upon a great stone, is a symbol of man controlling the ores and Elements of the Earth, and using his intelligence to shape and (eventually) wield them. This is true Dragon mastery — an idea made more pertinent by the dragon/serpent/phallic imagery inherent within the sword. Pulling the sword from the stone "proved" Arthur's kingship on outer levels to the massed lesser kings, but it was not confirmed on inner levels until he had been given Excalibur.

Again, it is Merlin who leads him to the appropriate lake in which Vivienne the Enchantress lives. The sword and its scabbard is given to the King by the Lady, who is seen as no more than an arm rising above the misty waters. In this tale, the sheer importance of the scabbard over that of the sword itself is emphasized. The sword can destroy, but the scabbard heals.

The sexual symbolism is obvious here again. The sword within the scabbard = the penis in the vagina = Man and Woman (and humanity) in perfect union.

Excalibur can therefore be seen as an image of the Dragon rising into the King's hand from the primeval depths. It can also be seen in a purely phallic sense, as the lost sexual organ of Osiris given back to the King to make him complete. It had been swallowed by a fish, remember, a singular aspect of the Piscean symbol for the present Age. It is given to him by the Lady of the Lake. However we choose to concentrate on specific images, the basis of the tale is that it is through Woman that Man can find himself, and all the healings that he might need.

Once this completion of the spirit is attained, he becomes "the divine man-child, the heir of eternity, self-begotten and self-born, King of Earth and Prince of the Underworld." These words apply exactly to the young Arthur at the moment when he accepts Excalibur, but they were written about Ra-Hera-khty, or Ra-Hoor-Khuit, as Ankh-f-n-Khonsu would have called him. Had Arthur been an Egyptian, he would have been granted the right to wear the crowns of the Upper and Lower Kingdoms at that moment, wield the crook and flail, wear the uraeus on his brow and become the exact balance to his predecessor, Osiris, in the Underworld just as Horus was in the outer world. As one descends into the Earth, the other soars into the sky. They balance each other in endless orbit.

Now comparative mythology is a dangerous topic for the dogmatist and pedant — especially those with what might be termed a qabalistic cast of mind. It is almost impossible, for example, to make one-to-one comparisons. There are extraordinary similarities between the Egyptian and Avalonian systems, but they are not *exactly* the same. The Mysteries of Egypt, for example, vibrate at a far slower frequency than those of Avalon. The Mysteries of Egypt established themselves and were fully recorded in various ways over thousands and thousands of years, while the Mysteries of Avalon were fragmented, distorted, and almost destroyed. So there will always be differences. Nevertheless, we can use the hard details of these two mythologies like pieces of flint: if we bring them together sharply enough, and at an appropriate angle, they will make sparks, they will bring Light. What we can see, so far, are themes of the Magical Mating, the Wondrous Child, and the idea of kingship that is ratified on divine levels but is yet intrinsically connected with the land.

Arthur, it should be seen, was a Triple figure in his own right as Child, Priest-King, and eventually Sacrificed God. It is at the juncture between leaving his Childhood and becoming a Priest-King that he receives Excalibur. It is from then on that he becomes, like Osiris in his "Green Man" aspect, inextricably linked and identified with the fertilities and fortunes of the kingdom he rules.

Arthur becomes High King then, and establishes himself at Camelot — the precise location of which is claimed exclusively by the Welsh, Scots, and English as being within their borders alone. Just as they all claim Arthur himself for their own, they also argue with scholarly brilliance and little agreement that the whole Cycle was an expression of the mysteries of their own particular nation. They support their arguments at all points with references to ancient texts, local place names, and legends. People outside the British Isles rarely appreciate the intensity with which the Welsh and Scots feel themselves to be nations apart, and only connected with that conglomerate known as Great Britain by circumstances of unhappy histories. Even within England, certain regions insist upon Arthurian locations of their own. The only truth can be that Camelot is a movable city. It is that area within our consciousness which is able to contain the figures of its myth. Camelot is an inner temple of vast size and splendor which we must all find within ourselves. Like Atlantis, like Arthur, Camelot is an essence. Take all the glamour from all the castles of Britain and Europe, all the glory from all the tales of chivalrous combat, then wrap them around some bleak and windswept hill-fort like the swathes around a mummy, and you have a place and a name which almost sings. Camelot is mankind looking back with nostalgia towards its infancy. Our childhood homes seem tinged with wonder, mysterious and scarcely comprehensible places which are always vast in the memory but unbelievably small and invariably decrepit when we visit them in reality as adults.

But however humble the kingdom and its capital, a King must necessarily have a Queen. A suitable wife was accordingly found by the name of Guinevere,

and brought with her, as her father's wedding gift, the
Round Table. The best knights in the world were to sit
around this. No man could sit at its head, and all were
equal with the King. In other words, they were a living
parallel to the Zodiac— intensely individual souls who
were, nevertheless, interacting parts of a corporate
whole. Merlin — again — inscribed each place with the
name of the knight who would occupy it. Their names
today provoke echoes of romance and pageantry that
are unequalled in the West: Galahad, Perceval and
Bors; Gareth, Gawaine and Gaheris...The list becomes too large for such a finite object as the Table had
to be. But then, it never existed on this plane at all. Of
them all, it was Galahad who would achieve the
greatest destiny on spiritual levels when he became one
of the two knights to attain the Holy Grail. Even so, for
a long time, the popular imagination held that his
father was really the best knight. This was Lancelot of
the Lake, who was soon to bring Camelot crashing
down for no other reason than that he loved too well ...

The name Guinevere comes from Gwenhwyfar,
which has been interpreted as "White Shadow" or
"White Phantom." This has obvious echoes with the
figure of Gwyn ap Nudd whom we will look at in the
next chapter, whose name means "Light Son of Darkness" — put the comma where you will. Gwynwhyfar
could equally be translated as "Light from the Shadow."
In this, can we find some hint of an initiatic name given
to the wife of the Horned God? We can if we want. It
might be a deliberate mistranslation, but it bears
magic.

She is in many ways the pivot of the Cycle — that
aspect which turns it toward tragedy rather than
triumph. In some ways she is Maat, bringing order and
pattern into the court (via the Round Table). In other

ways, she is the representative of the Earth in Spring.

> ... the fecundity maiden who has to be fertilized
> that the earth shall bring forth joy and abundance,
> This is the story of the Mother Earth, first as a fair
> maiden, the May Queen in white or pale green,
> crowned with flowers, the magical virgin with
> whom the God or hero mates to bring back the
> Earth to fertility ... Then the maiden becomes the
> bountiful matron of the fruits of the Earth in har-
> vest time.[7]

But, to the dismay of all, Guinevere proved completely infertile when it came to the crucial matter of
providing the country with another Pendragon to
perpetuate the Cycle. However, she did something
which was to affect the whole of her world and worlds to
come. What she did was quite extraordinary. There
would be nothing like it in Europe with quite the same
impact — not until the English yeomen mastered the
use of the longbow to slaughter the entire nobilities of
France, or Patton's army swept across the Carentan
Peninsula and flamed its way toward Berlin, or until a
large and strange cloud was seen above Alamogordo in
1944, at the ending and beginning of an Age. What
Guinivere did was quite simple: she fell in love, In some
ways, she took us all with her.

It is generally held these days that the idealization of
love, and the concept of Romantic Love, were not
something that had existed since the beginning of Time,
but were in fact brought into something of a flowering
only as recently as the 11th and 13th centuries through
the influence of the Troubadors, Minnesingers, and all
those writers and storytellers who developed the
concept. Prior to that, whatever considerable feelings a

man might hold for his woman was always completely subsidiary to his loyalty for and duty toward his lord. Nothing would or should come before that. So what happened between Lancelot and Guinevere was almost unbelievable, staggering. It does not matter that they may never have existed as historical personages. Their images are real enough within the dream-world of the psyche at least. The story of that romance helped awaken within women — and not a few men — the possibility that there could be more to a husband and wife relationship than mere childbearing.

No, Guinevere had no earthly child, but on other levels she gave birth to Love instead.

In the romance *Perceval le Gallois,* she is in fact shown in greater depth than the popular tales allow:

> . . . there has never been a lady of such renown ... for, just as the wise master teaches young children, my lady the queen teaches and instructs every living being. From her flows all the good in the world, she is its source and origin. Nobody can take leave of her and go away disheartened for she knows what each person wants and the way to please each according to his desires. Nobody observes the way of Rectitude or wins honour unless they have done so from my lady, or can suffer such distress that he leaves her still possessed of his grief.

If Arthur is to be associated with Osiris, can we see echoes of Isis within Guinevere? Only so much as we can see Isis in *all* women. In other respects, the answer has to be no. After all, Isis' love was for her brother, keeping it in the family as did many noble families throughout the world. Isis is perhaps not the best one to follow or invoke when you first fall in love: She comes to cope with the problems that inevitably follow after this initial state. Guinevere, in contrast, comes to us from the start. She is even there *before* the start of any love match. She has not yet come into her own.

Guinevere

So she fell in love with Lancelot, and he loved her in return to the point of madness, almost torn apart by this and his duty toward his beloved King. It was this love which brought the whole of Camelot and the Realm tumbling down. Like Osiris, the Holy Realm of Logres was to be torn apart, and bits of the magical edifices scattered all over the known world.

In many ways, the importance of the Arthurian Cycle

is to be found in the matings and the marriages — and in the children that were or were not born as a result. There was Elaine, daughter of that Fisher-King who ruled the wasteland and guarded the Holy Grail. She pretended to be Guinevere one dark night and tricked Lancelot into sleeping with her — much as Nephthys slept with Osiris. The result of the union was Galahad, the pure and perfect youth who was to find that Holy Grail. There was Morgan le Fay, the great Witch-Queen who used magic in order to sleep with her half-brother, Arthur, in an echo both of Nephthys again and of the brother-sister matings among the pharaohs. Both Elaine and Morgan were "magical" women with peculiar Otherworld associations. It is almost as though the unforseen sterility of Guinevere forced the priesthood that worked behind the scenes to find other ways of perpetuating the Pendragon Mysteries — not for their own purposes, but to ensure the continuation of the land's fertility and life on all levels. It all devolved upon those concepts: The land and its people are one and the King and the Land are One. As it was, through the resulting children of Galahad and Mordred, the whole Cycle was taken into some completely unexpected directions.

The Round Table was, and is, a symbol of universal order — more so now in this era of detente and interminable summits than ever before. Camelot was almost like a cross section of some great world axis; it was the center of the nation, radiating its energies outward. In the light of those two axioms quoted above, an ordered, balanced, and harmonious court would mean the same thing in village, town, district, and kingdom.

The actual image of a Round Table does not appear in Ancient Egypt — unless you count the circular

passage of the sun across the Earth and through the
Underworld — but the concept behind it does. In fact,
the whole land was a manifestation of the concept:

> . . . the sacred geography of ancient Egypt corre-
> sponded precisely with the realms of the dead, so
> that the 42 provinces of the Upper and Lower
> Kingdoms mirrored the 42 provinces of the Judges
> of the Dead, the Upper Gods of the Orbit, and the
> Lower Gods of the Horizon. And all of these were
> mirrored in the Great Pyramid, the "House of the
> Hidden Places," so that when the initiate com-
> pleted his journey through the labyrinths of the
> Pyramid of Light, and had emerged above, illu-
> mined, he had therefore simultaneously mastered
> and transcended all the worlds, which were mir-
> rored within the Pyramid itself.[8]

As above, so below; as without, so within.

Intriguingly, We can catch glimpses of this in Britain
too in circular Earth-zodiacs that more and more
researchers are finding in the topography of various
regions. These zodiacs are formed by the natural
features of the land, and are only perceivable from the
air or on detailed maps, and are invariably linked with
local mystery centers of vast age and sanctity. The most
famous of these is at Glastonbury in Somerset. This is a
town with more Arthurian associations than most.

Guinevere, then, as the Royal Queen, helped bring
this sense of order and pattern to the court both via the
stability that any Queen should bring to a kingdom and
also through the Round Table that was brought along
with her. This is the significance of the throne symbol
which appears in the tarot card known as The Empress.
Guinevere, as the constructive force within Nature and
society, encouraged the tradition-oriented cohesion of

the collective. Through her establishment in the court, conditions were created in which the institutions of law and order could take root. After that, a pattern of learning and spiritual ethics were laid down which would allow the quality of mercy to modify and shape the otherwise ferocious militarism of the Table's members. Guinivere, in brief, was the power of womanhood in the process of creating civilization.

For a time it all went wondrously well. Arthur was a just and strong ruler; the court became the center of small miracles. Magical harts, Green Knights, and ladies in distress appeared, which lured individual knights off on quests that would test their prowess and their goodness and add to the splendor of Camelot. It was only after some time that Arthur suspected what the rest of the court had long known — that the Queen was in love with his champion; that Guinevere was in love with Lancelot. Forces were unleashed that tore society apart — forces every bit as luminous and devastating as those which arise in splitting the atom.

Today, we might learn to use those forces in a process of fusion rather than fission. We can learn to reconstruct ourselves with them — and our futures also.

The key to much of the magic discussed or alluded to in the present book is to be found in the figure of Lancelot of the Lake, son of Ban of Benoic. Benoic is a place most usually regarded as being in France but which is often claimed by the Scots as theirs. Scots claim most things to be theirs, however. Thomas Malory gives the seat of Lancelot's power as Bamburgh Castle in Northumberland, the north-easternmost region of England. This was the original Castle Dolorous which Lancelot himself renamed Joyous Gard, after falling in love. Clearly, he was a man with high hopes for this new love affair.

Lancelot was without doubt the most formidable fighting man of his time — or of any time. No one could defeat him in combat by fair means or foul. Strong beyond compare, gallant to an hypnotic degree, brave to the point of madness, and also humble, gentle, and utterly devoted to the King. He was, they all knew, "the best knight in the world." He is what all men would imagine themselves to be at heart, in essence, in some way. Like Horus, his time is not yet arrived — not quite.

Like Horus, too, he is raised and taught to fight by Women of Magic; in this case, by the Lady of the Lake — the same one who had given Arthur the sword Excalibur — and who must be seen as something akin to the Queen of Faery. The mystic ladies who grouped themselves around this Queen taught the strange young boy all that he needed to know about the arts of war in a clear parallel to Horus' upbringing in the marshes of the Delta where Isis and Nephthys brought him up to challenge and defeat Set. In both cases, there are dim memories evoked of an obscure Celtic tradition that it was once women, not men, who first taught boys the skills of war.

If the romance between Lancelot and Guinevere can be regarded as something of a prophetic dream — for the race, rather than the individual — then it is the Troubadors whom we must thank for giving voice and words to such dreams. Men and women, they were more than mere singers wandering from castle to castle; they were vibrant expressions of an attitude and emotion completely new to the times in which they lived. In the courts of what we now know as France, they created an atmosphere of culture and amenity toward womankind which nothing had hitherto approached. Their songs were heavily perfumed with those Gnostic or Dualist philsophies the Roman Church would soon do its best to destroy. So they created this mode of "courtly love" that gradually altered the whole shape of Western civilization. Whether they simply expressed a current that was welling up within the psyche or whether their movement initiated that current is a matter for debate. Certainly Jehane de Notredame was sufficiently impressed by them to write a history in the year 1575, some 400 years or more later, entitled *Vies des plus celebres at anciens poetes provensaux.* He also attempted some history molding himself when he wrote his famous propheices under the name Nostradamus.

It was a man from this tradition, Chretien de Troyes, whom we have to consider in any analysis of the Arthurian Cycle. After all, Lancelot did not appear until 1170 when Chretien mentioned him in the list of Arthur's knights in his work *Erec.* It is he who first mentions that knight's love for Guinevere, and we first hear of the Holy Grail from him. Apparently working under the patronage of Eleanor of Aquitaine, it is Chretien who was largely responsible for recording some images that we are still following today, like markings on a dusty road.

But there is a curious aspect to the literary figure of Lancelot. If we are to grab him by the shoulders and turn him around, we find that, like Janus, he faces two ways. The face to the rear is indeed that of another knight entirely. It is the face of Gawaine.

The name Gawaine is derived either from *Gwalchmai* or *Gwalchwyn,* meaning the Hawk of May or the White Hawk, respectively. Robert Graves regarded them as decidedly mystical names, while Jessie Weston advanced the theory that Gawaine was the first Grail winner. Perhaps in this context the White Hawk is a decidedly coy translation: let us make him into the Hawk of Light instead.

Lancelot

It is almost as if Gawaine is Lancelot's alter-ego. Chretien, for example, often uses Gawaine to make contrasts with du Lac, as Lancelot is often called. In the unfinished *Le Conte du Graal* (unfinished because Chretien was burned to death in mysterious circumstances), the two knights undertake parallel adventures. The difference is that Gawaine does not seek the Grail itself but for the bleeding Lance which drips into it. Some authorities tend to dismiss Lancelot entirely as no more than an extended version of Gawaine, and point out that in some sources it is the latter who becomes Guinevere's lover, not du Lac. But there is more to it than that.

What seems to have happened is that Gawaine, a fine knight, became regarded as a symbol of what could be achieved by martial prowess and physical strength. Lancelot, however, became an expanded symbol to show what he could and should have achieved, not through strength alone but through power and love conjoined. Gawaine fails in the "Queste del Saint Graal" because he relies exclusively on prowess, refuses to seek the help of divine grace, and remains blind to the spiritual significance of the Grail. It is Lancelot who has come to progress further spiritually; it is Lancelot who most inspires our affections. Perhaps it is most accurate to say that du Lac was created as Gawaine's higher self. It was Lancelot who was created as a symbol through which we could invoke a peculiar quality of love in the ages to come.

So let us go a step further and say that the avatar of the Aeon of Horus, as Ankh-f-n-Khonsu called this Age more commonly known as the Age of Aquarius (the Water-carrier), will be Gawaine/ Lancelot: the Hawk of May and the great du Lac.

There are indications of this in the so-called Gnostic Gospels:

> But when the nature of mankind has been taken up and a generation of men moved by my voice comes close to me, thou (John) who hearest me now, wilt have become the same and that which is will no longer be.

This, from the apocryphal Acts of John, alludes to the tradition that at the end of our Age it will be John, the beloved disciple, who will be raised to become the next light-bringer. Of course, the John-equivalent in the Arthurian Cycle is clearly Lancelot — for which knight was more beloved of Arthur than Lancelot? The very essence of the tragedy is that this great knight loved his King beyond all men — but his Queen beyond life itself. The moral dilemma tore him apart and drove him to madness and set him off along the path of what Joseph Campbell describes as Separation, Initiation, and Return. He became a forest-dweller, a wild man confronting demons in the wilderness of his pscyhe. If Arthur, in one of the Welsh poems, made a descent into the Underworld to win a cauldron — a sort of proto-Grail — then Lancelot did much the same through his love for Guinevere. Lancelot was, and is, the wish-fulfillment of the Western spirit, an incarnation of Love and Power. He is the god-form of the New Age — a telesmic image born out of the ruins of Mordred (of whom more presently) based upon Gawaine, and deliberately created to enable consciousness to function on certain lines. Lancelot never existed in the historical sense, but everyone contains his foetus within his or her subconscious, locked away behind that symbol for the Underworld ⊗, floating and dreaming within the amniotic fluid of his or her dreams.[9]

It was a mysterious mating between du Lac and Elaine (daughter of the Osiris-like Fisher King) which produced Galahad, one of the two Grail winners, whose chastity and purity enabled them to leave this realm entirely and spend infinities within some Christian heaven. Lancelot, in contrast, although granted a vision of the Grail Ceremony, was denied the full attainment because of his sins with Guinevere. Sins? As an old and dying man, his final confession began: "I have loved a Queen beyond compare, and I have loved

her an exceedingly long time . . ." Confession? It is a
hymn to love. Who could care about two virginal little
prigs like Galahad and Perceval when there is a figure
like du Lac to aspire toward? Lancelot turns his back on
the sterile heaven of the Christian Grail and becomes a
Western *bodhisattva,* in essence.

To appreciate him a bit more, however, we must look
more closely at his alter-ego of Gawaine, as a version of
Horus. According to the magician Kenneth Grant, who
has long worked directly with the Magical Currents
intiated by Ankh-f-n-Khonsu:

> The Horus-hawk . . . represents the power of trans-
> cending earth. Its terrestrial shadow is symbolised
> by the dragon . . . the beast that devours the solar
> god . . .[10]

We know already that Gawaine is the Hawk of May,
or the Hawk of Light; we read that his strength waxes
before noon, wanes after it; we know about his
connection with the Pendragon, who is in fact his uncle;
and we can see his connection with Lancelot when we
find that the only traceable meaning for that name is
from a Germanic root meaning "land." Further,
Gawaine bore the device of the pentagram upon his
shield, while this same symbol is a positive attribution
of Horus. The words Horus and Aries may reflect one
another. Additionally, we learn that Aries in the zodiac
also represents that Green Man, the "Vernal Power of
the Sun," which links us with the story of the Green
Knight that is so vital to Gawaine. Again, there is the
tradition that power is passed down through the sister's
son, on the principle that the purity of the blood-line is
thus certain — and Gawaine is nephew to the King on
his mother's side.

Gawaine's Star

It is via his mystical adventure with the Green Knight, however, that we glide almost effortlessly back into the realms of pure Osirian symbolism. The basic story is described in a superbly evocative, alliterative epic poem of unknown authorship entitled *Sir Gawain and the Green Knight*. It goes as follows:

On New Year's Day, a gigantic knight appears in Arthur's court, clad entirely in green, riding a green horse. He proposes a bargain whereby any one of the King's knights may strike off his head with the axe he carries providing that the same knight will accept a return blow in a year's time. Gawaine takes up the challenge and is astonished to see the Green Knight pick up his head after being decapitated, order Gawaine to meet him at the Green Chapel at the stipulated time, and then gallop off with his head under his arm.

The next Christmas sees Gawaine in a vast and dreary forest looking for the Green Chapel. The lord of a nearby castle offers him hospitality for the remaining days before his rendezvous, telling his that the chapel in question is only a few miles distant. The lord also

makes a stipulation: he will go hunting each day while
Gawaine remains at the castle with his wife. At the end
of each day, they will exchange their spoils. While the
lord is out hunting, however, his lovely wife comes into
Gawaine's room and tries to seduce him. Our knight,
conscious of duty and honor toward his host, will do no
more than let her kiss him. When the lord comes back
and presents the venison he has caught to Gawaine, the
latter gives him a kiss, his "spoils" for that day. The
second day, the same thing happens, Gawaine trading
another kiss for a boar. But, on the third day, the lady
insists on giving him her green, golden-hemmed girdle,
which this time Gawaine keeps secret, exchanging a
third kiss for the fox that the lord has caught. The next
day, Gawaine sets out for his appointed meeting and
duly meets the Green Knight next to one of the
chambered tombs known as "barrows":

> It had a hole in each end and on either side,
> And was overgrown with grass in great patches.
> All hollow it was within, only an old cavern
> Or the crevice of an ancient crag . . .

True to the conditions, Gawaine lays his head upon
the block — only for the giant to take two mock blows,
which not unnaturally unnerve Gawaine somewhat.
Steeling himself to receive the third and fatal blow, he
is exulted to feel the blade do no sore than nick the side
of his neck. Having fulfilled his promise and lived, he
springs up joyfully to find that the Green Knight and
his recent host are one and the same, and the cut he
received at the third stroke was his punishment for
stealing the girdle. The giant goes on to explain that his
name is Bertilak of the High Desert, and that the lady
in his castle is none other than Morgan le Fay,

Gawaine's aunt. The whole adventure has been a magical test, not only for himself as an individual, but also for the spirit behind the whole Round Table.

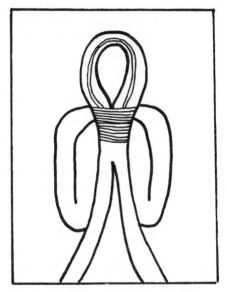

The tat *(buckle or knot of Isis)*

Now, like a Sufi tale, the true meaning of this is a secret between God and the individual interpretation of each reader. But, in broad terms, we can catch glimpses within this story of the head-cult that was common throughout Celtic society, of solar heroes, fertility rites — all spiced up with Troubador ethics of courtly love. But, underneath these glimpses, we can find the enduring image of Osiris in his aspect of Vegetation God, as the Corn King losing his head to be born again next year. The Green Knight is the cyclical aspect of Nature, or death and renewal, but he is also Osiris challenging Horus and testing his worthiness to suc-

ceed him. There are the Osirian parallels of the
dwelling mound, the desert land in which he lives, the
girdle (which represents the *tat,* or "girdle" of Isis) the
axe which parallels the adze (an image of the constellation of the Great Bear) that Horus used for the
ceremony of the Opening of the Mouth that caused
fertility to burst forth once more. As regards that
girdle/garter, there is also William Gray's comment
relating to Venus, the planet of Love:

> To control Venus, the secret of her Zona, or girdle,
> had to be known. It was tied with a special knot,
> and its pattern hid the secret. Once this was mas-
> tered, Love came under control of Will, for the knot
> could be fastened or unfastened according to the
> Initiate's intention.[11]

As Ankh-f-n-Khonsu said: "Love is the law, love
under will."

We shall return to Lancelot and Gawaine later, and
in more ways than one, for they are the Celtic images of
the New Aeon under whose aegis we might learn to
work. They are levels of consciousness which we can
choose to explore within ourselves and thus stimulate
similar levels in the consciousness of humanity as a
whole. But first we must press on to that final part
within the Arthurian Cycle in which his role as
Priest-King gives way to his inevitable glory as Sacrificed God.

The basic events are simple enough. Arthur's bastard
son, Mordred, comes to Camelot and takes his place in
court. At the Feast of Pentecost, a marvelous vision of
the Holy Grail appears before the knights of the Round
Table. This vessel was widely regarded as the cup out of
which Christ drank at the Last Supper, but which has

many echoes of Celtic cauldron myths from earlier periods. In itself, the vision turns the feast into something of a Last Supper also, for all the knights then depart in quest of the Grail. But someone should have warned them; they should never have gone. It was the effective end of order within the court.

The Round Table begins to fall apart. Gradually, Mordred engineers things so that Arthur is forced to admit that he has been "given the horns," as was once said — cuckolded by his best friend. Lancelot is caught in bed with the Queen, but manages to flee the trap. Guinevere is brought to trial and found guilty under Arthur's own laws. As she is about to be burnt to death, Lancelot mounts a rescue and carries her off to Bamburgh. Eventually Guinevere goes back to Arthur of her own accord, but the King lays siege to his former champion's castle. Meanwhile, Guinevere is then abducted by Mordred, who proclaims himself as King. Arthur withdraws his troops from Bamburgh and pursues Mordred's army.

Finally, at the battle of Camlann, the two armies wipe each other out, and the mortally wounded King is helped to the shore of a lake by Sir Bedivere. After some persuasion, Sir Bedivere throws the sword Excalibur out into the lake, where a lady's arm rises as before and takes it to its proper place. Arthur, mortally wounded, is last seen carried off in a magic barge, attended by three Queens, on his journey to the mystic Isle of Avalon. There he waits, not dead but not really alive, until the time comes when Britain faces deadly peril again . . .

That is a bare retelling of some of the most poignant events in literary history, but it will do for a start. Let us look at some of the more esoteric aspects now.

Mordred was a bastard. The bastard son of Arthur by his half-sister Morgan le Fay, the Witch-Queen of the Britons and Bretons. Morgan, as noted, used her magical powers to trick her step-brother into sleeping with her, which immediately gives her a link with Nephthys in her Celtic aspect. As stepsister to Arthur, her mating corresponds directly to those between the pharaoh and his sister, the intention being the preservation or strengthening of a sacred blood-line. Mordered, it was hoped, would be a Wonder-child just as his father had been.

Magicians almost uniformly agree that Morgan (sometimes said to mean "sea-born") was the title given to a high priestess of Atlantean origin, the direct counterpart of the Merlin. This is the sea-priestess who came to the western shores in order to teach men the ways of the Moon, the powers of the sea, and the secrets of sacred bloodlines. Now this "occult eugenics" or selective breeding is something repugnant to us today — in part because of those energies released by Guinevere — but in an Aeon when humanity was by no means as individuated as now, when communities had a much more herd-like collective consciousness, these practices were a means of making links with evolutionary energies on inner levels. In time, via the nature of those Sacred Kings who used and understood these energies, the benefit was passed on to the people as a whole.

The cycle contains one long story in which Morgan manages to steal the scabbard of Excalibur from the King for a brief while. Beneath the Christian gloss of these tales, and determined attempts to give Morgan some purely evil attributes, we can find within this act traces of a struggle between the patriarchal systems which eventually dominated the West and those

Mysteries of Women which they superseded. Morgan wanted the healing scabbard because, as a woman, it was hers by right, and because she found herself fighting a Kingship that had lost its balance and thus tried to appropriate everything to the masculine. The scabbard was the talisman of the proto-witches; healing was their province, their magic. But an unbalanced masculinity was trying to keep it for its sole use, aided and abetted by a Christian Church which found the idea of any kind of fertility cult pure anathema. Hence the Christian scribe/interpreter's insistence that the winners of the Grail were chaste virgins. Ridiculous as it may sound, this was a little notion which survived the centuries, so that magicians and occultists of all persuasions, even until comparatively recent decades, remained convinced that spiritual attainment was proportionate to sexual abstinence. Although that was one attitude Ankh-f-n-Khonsu never shared. No one was going to make him keep *his* pants on. And in many curious ways, he helped smooth the way for witches of today to reclaim that inner talisman of the scabbard and to use it in its proper manner. All this came about because of the battles fought by Morgan and her kind upon the outer and the inner planes.

Her son Mordred, on the other hand, is what might be termed a Triple God figure. The others in his trinity would be Lancelot and Gawaine. Being son and nephew to the King, his very birth was attended by portents. Merlin had prophesied that Arthur would be killed by a person born on Mayday, the ancient Celtic feast of Beltain. And so the King ordered all children born of nobility on the day in question to be put to death. The method of execution involved putting the babes on board a ship and sending it to sea and certain shipwreck. When the inevitable happened, Mordred was the only survivor, being washed ashore where he was found and looked after by a good man. There are obvious Biblical echoes here, and we are reminded too of the Welsh bard Taliesin being set adrift in a coracle— much the same as happened to Anubis, too.

In some ways Mordred is like Set; he was the victim of a bad press. Mordred is that energy which stops a man becoming set in his ways. Or: Mordred is that energy which stops a man from becoming Set in his ways. It is a play upon words, but there is wisdom to be gleaned from it nevertheless.

In one sense, Mordred aptly fits into the role of Lord of Justice — a British Thoth in balance with the Hermes and Anubis of Gawaine and Lancelot, respectively. Although, like all Triple Gods, the qualities can change like alternating currents. But the Set comparison is more appropriate in the way that he challenges Arthur for the Kingship, much as Set challenged first Osiris and then Horus for the same. In some tales, it is Mordred who elopes with Guinevere in an act of mutual complicity. In these tales, he is far removed from the malignant and cowardly traitor that the popular imagination casts him as being.

What we must realize is that Osiris (and thus Everyman) actually *becomes* Set when he tries to hang onto his power. Women are best able to understand this. A woman loses a peculiar type and quality of power — her fertility — during the menopause, and then must learn to seek a different kind of fertility, and one which is not related to bearing children. It is not a fate that afflicts man's sperm, obviously, but he too must learn to give way, and let go, in completely different areas. The temporal power of the male over his own realm does not necessarily have to become corrupt — there are ways to avoid this — but it *always* becomes corrupt when he seeks to perpetuate this power for the length of his days. There are things man must learn to yield to, not least of which are the needs of his wife and children — who are growing just as much as he. The times when this yielding is most appropriate must also be learned. Like the Osirian corn-dollies, with barley pushing up through the framework, all men must allow their dependants to grow through them, and glorify him in that way.

Mordred understood that. In magical terms, his is the disruptive energy which perpetually breaks up and destroys all forms. He breaks up and destroys — but he also sets free. He also Sets free. These acts of destruction, when performed by a Sacrifical Priest, can produce energy which will, as Dion Fortune says in *The Sea Priestess,* "re-appear on the planes of form as an entirely different type of force to that as which it started." So the power behind the Arthurian Cycle — power which was in danger of being ossified through its complacency — was actually transmuted by Mordred and then stored until the day it would be needed again. He destroyed the old order based upon the sort of "selective breeding" that was valid for that time and type of consciousness. This is all too appallingly reminiscent of the Nazi *Lebensborn* program, which included human stud farms aimed at creating a super race. He destroyed this order by bringing out into the open those energies flowing through Guinevere, whom he helps to balance.

Mordred, Gawaine, and Lancelot are, then, aspects of one type of energy perhaps best associated with the planet Mars, in astrological terms. They counterbalance the trinity of Guinevere, Morgan le Fay, and Elaine (associated with the planet Jupiter). The Triple

God and these Three Queens form what we might think of as the two wings of the Dragon. Within them are are to be the qualities which will enable the serpent-powers to uncoil themselves and rise up from their abode — whether this is in the Tuat, the underground cave, or that chakra at the base of the spine associated with the kundalini. Through them the serpent energies are given both lift and direction; with wings, the serpent becomes a dragon and can fly. It is a rising and a flight based upon an interchange of energies for which sexual union is a low level analog and also a primary key. It is the sort of interchange hinted at, in crude form, by the exchange of gifts between Gawaine and the Green Knight. These are the energies involved in working with Ankh-f-n-Khonsu's famous dictum "Love is the law, love under will," which in itself prevents his "Do what thou wilt shall be the whole of the Law" from being solely an expression of might is right.

Before we go on to completely new fields, we might take one final look at the concept of Guinevere from the Egyptian viewpoint and so tie up some loose ends in this comparative mythology.

The clearest parallel to her can be found in the image of Hathor, whose role oscillates between that of Isis, as protectress and defender of women's rights, and Sekhmet, the lioness deity who cannot be appeased once she has tasted blood. Hathor's name seems to mean "House of the Face." This was initially a cow's face, but was later likened to a sistrum. The name Horus was derived from the same root, and so Hathor became closely associated with him. In later stages of her cult, it was customary for the Queen of Egypt to identify herself with Hathor and lead the other priest-esses in the temple rituals devoted to Horus and the other gods. She was the goddess of music and dancing and light-hearted pleasures, and she was the Goddess of Love — that most of all. The Troubadors, railing against a time when the masculine had for too long been exalted at the expense of the feminine, would have adored Hathor.

Hathor as
Horned Goddess

Because of her natural connections with fertility, she often overlapped with Isis as regards the rising of the Nile and the Dog-star, Sothis. She is indeed the Horned Goddess, the Lady of the Sycamore Tree which some traditions insist was the tree that grew up around Osiris' body after it had been washed ashore at Byblos. She was the goddess who suckled dead souls, and in the Late Period while a dead man was still called an Osiris, dead women were Hathors — which again shows that these names were as much titles or descriptions of function as anything personal.

> Hathor was represented as a star-spangled cow, as a woman with a broad human or sistrum-shaped head and cow's ears or wearing a solar disk between the horns. She is most often seen with a sistrum as goddess of joy; suckling the living or dead; or as Goddess of the West, standing on the mountain of the West to welcome the dying sun into her arms — a combination of her solar and Osirian characteristics.[12]

In another world, another time, another stratum of consciousness, the Horned Gods of Europe would have recognised her as their own true consort. As our imagination flickers back and forth between the images of Gwenhwyfar and Hathor, one charging up the other in a kind of synergistic exchange, we can see how she can cross both worlds and both times as the Lady of the Sycamore — a title that could have come from any

Maat, wearing her symbol of the feather

of the witch-cults. If the Horned God of the West, who is the true subject of this book, can be seen to ride from the darkness between the trees (that fecund darkness within which the seeds of life and light germinate), then she is to be found *within* the trees themselves, emanating love and law — or *maat*. Soon, we will learn to talk with her. This, really, is all her husband has ever wanted us to do . . .

Notes

[1]There is an attitude current among English magicians which asserts that the personality and all its details is unimportant, or at best irrelevant, and that we must concern ourselves solely with the philsophies and concepts behind it. This may very well be true on levels of the advanced magical arts, but on all human levels it is a stiff and stuffy kind of wisdom.

[2]Normandi Ellis, *Awakening Osiris.* (Grand Rapids, MI: Phanes Press, 1988), p. 23.

[3]J. P. Cohane, "The Key," quoted by John Iviny in *The Sphinx and the Megaliths.* (London: 1974), p.?

[4] Carr Collins and Charles Fielding, *The Story of Dion Fortune.* (New York: Star and Cross Publications, 1985), p. 135.

[5]Ithell Colquhoun, *The Sword of Wisdom.* (London: Neville Spearman, 1975). This book contains what few details are about the relationship between the Druid Universal Bond and the Hermetic Order of the Golden Dawn.

[6]Ian Richardson, *Priestess, the Life and Magic of Dion Fortune.* (Wellingborough, UK: Aquarian Press, 1986).

[7]Veronica Ions, *Egyptian Mythology.* (London: Newnes Books, 1965), p. 112.

[8]Arthur Versluis, *The Egyptian Mysteries,* (London: Arkana, 1988), p. 76.

[9]There are strong links here with Harsaphes (or Herishef), a local God of Heracleopolis Magna in the Faiyum. Harsaphes was a ram-deity represented by a ram-headed man. He was a God of Fertility connected with water, and his name means "He who is on the Lake." As a national deity he was considered to be a specialized form of Horus.

[10]Kenneth Grant, *Aleister Crowley and the Hidden God.* (London: Muller, 1973).

[11]W. G. Gray, *The Ladder of Lights.* (Toddington, UK: Helios, 1968), p. 81.

[12]Ions, *op. cit.,* p. 82.

The Caves and Forests

The Horned God comes from the darkness — that curious, living, intensely aware darkness which exists within the forest, between the trees, and through which the shafts of light roar down to form the columns of some great arboreal cathedral. The Horned God, who is, of course, the presiding deity within this cathedral, was well-known to the early Celts who made their homes on the edge of those vast forests that once covered most of Europe — and most of the world.

We find him in Rheims, where an image survives which shows him holding a large bag from which pours a stream of coins, while below him lurk a bull and a stag. These figures might be regarded as his true courtiers. We find him in Paris, on the Pilier des Nautes, where his upper body has survived on otherwise damaged stonework. This shows him with upward pointing horns, from each of which hangs a torc. He also has two pairs of ears — one human and the other animal. On the Gundestrup cauldron, which can be seen in the National Museum at Copenhagen, he is seen

with his splendid antlers, surrounded by wild beasts
which include a wolf and a stag. He is also holding a
ram-headed serpent in his left hand. In a similar vein,
on a cross-shaft at Clonmacnois in Ireland, he is
portrayed grasping two wolves by their tails. At Val
Camonica in Italy, on a very old rock carving indeed, he
is shown as a tall standing figure with antlers and what
may be torcs — symbols of authority — on his arms. On
a small plaque in the Corinium Museum at Cirencester
in England, he is shown holding a serpent in each hand.
A similar bronze figure was found in the same region at
Southbroom in Wiltshire, where the God is standing
and again holds ram-headed serpents, which coil
around his legs. And there is a Pictish carving from
Meigle in Perthshire, Scotland, which depicts a horned
deity holding an intricate pattern of coils derived from a
pair of serpents and with coiling legs ending in
fish-tails. Even to the most sober and non-mystical
commentator:

> The Celts clearly saw him as an earth god of fertil-
> ity and plenty. The snake symbolizes the life-force
> and powers of regeneration, hence its representa-
> tion on the staff of Aesculapius and the caduceus of
> Mercury. It is only in the Garden of Eden that the
> serpent became evil.[1]

But perhaps the first known representation is within
the Caverne des Trois Freres in the Ariege, which some
sources estimate dates back 30,000 years or more. To
call this particular image a Horned God, however, is
something of a misnomer in this instance because it is
clearly a man clothed in the skin of a stag, and wearing
its antlers, so that his whole body is covered by the
animal's hide. His head and feet are clearly seen as

though the material were transparent. So it is obviously the intention of the artist to show us that here, in that awkward and difficult part of the cave used for part of some initiatory rite or teaching, was a priest fully possessed by his God.

From Le Caverne des Trois Freres, Ariege

Another image, from the Fourneau du Diable, is shown not only dancing, but also accompanying himself with an instrument variously described as a kind of musical bow or even a flute. Decide for yourself. In all cases these images indicate a time when the priesthood and its priestesses would invoke their totemic spirits with the help of ritual masks.

Now this is not "primitive" magic, but rather a technique that was used consistently throughout the Egyptian Mysteries, and within many of those religions

and cults that sprang up around the Mediterranean.
There is a temple painting from Denderah which shows
a priest wearing the mask of Anubis being led to a
religious ceremony. The use of masks in Greek and
Roman ritual dramas is well documented, while, at the
other side of the known world, masks were vital to those
Mysteries of Mithras practiced throughout Roman
Britain. Indeed, within the ruined Temple of Mithras at
Carrawburgh, along Hadrian's Wall, it is still possible
to catch disconcerting glimpses of the astral forms of
those officiants who took their places within the niches
along each wall — each one resplendent in the
appropriate human or animal mask. Further afield
still, among the American Indians, we find wooden

Dancer, from the Fourneau du Diable, Dordogne

masks representing simple elemental forces such as the
Spirit of the Wind, or Cold Weather. The Kwakuitl
tribes of British Columbia created sophisticated masks.
These incorporated mechanical devices through which
the shaman could give himself a new face during the
ritual dances, and create the maximum effect.

Egyptian priest wearing the jackal mask

We could posit several major masks within the
natural realm: the Mask of the Raven, associated with
Saturn; the Mask of the Dove, which relates to Jupiter;
that of the Hawk, which can be used to invoke the forces
of Mars. Then there is the Mask of the Royal Stag of the
Sun, on whose antlers birds perch; the Cow (or Bull) of
Venus; the Mask of the Fox, for Mercury; the Mask of
the Hare of the Moon — and the Mask of the Earth
Serpent. These represent a broad spectrum of consciousness that can be tapped with the aid of the
tutelary deities concerned. These deities are, in a sense,

the Higher Aspects of familiars beloved by witches. Sometimes, instead of masks, suggestive symbols were used — black feathers in the hair, pelts, antlered helmets — all of these were backed up by the vitality of natural locations, huge fires, light from the heavens, songs, chants, clapping, and drums — those great drums that can make the earth shake and force you to follow their beat no matter what. But in each case the real work was done by the actual human who was channelling these forces — male or female. Great actors and mime artists have an uncanny talent for becoming greater than themselves, projecting such semi-illusions not solely by mere technique but by the inner assumption of animal "essence."

In this sanitized world, we have too easily chosen to ignore or scorn the effect of masks. In the negative sense, they can create an air of maliciousness and menace to make even the puniest villains seem filled with power. Masks obliterate the human personality with all its frail quirks, all its physiological imperfections. Made properly and used with skill on highly charged occasions, the effect upon the consciousness of the celebrants can be staggering. Holes can be punched in the rational defenses, and the candidate for initiation can be made to know that he is, beyond any doubt, in the company of gods. From the operator's point of view, masks can, by subduing the vitally important sense of smell, create the sense that what is being seen is not truly three-dimensional, not truly happening to the mundane personality at all. By suppressing the impact of one dimension, masks allow the interaction with other dimensions in its place.

We have already noted Osiris' role as a Horned God and seen how his qualities were vital to the theocratic culture of Egypt over enormous periods of time. In other cult centers along the Nile, it was Amon, originally a local deity of Thebes, who took on the Osirian head-gear in this respect. Generally, the goddesses wore the horns of cattle while the gods were adorned with the horns of sheep or rams. Thus a priest of Amon would wear the curved horns of the Theban ram and ram's skin over his shoulders in much the same way that the dancing man of the Ariege was wrapped within skins of his own. Far from being the "primitive" religious expression of a hunting/gathering Stone Age culture, this assumption of animal forms, in one way or another, was fundamental to the deepest practices of all cultures at that time.

But I would go a step further and predict that occult historians in a century's time will look back upon this decade as the moment when the scattered parts of the dismembered Western Mystery Tradition were finally reconstructed, all save one piece. When that piece is found (and it will be soon), when the shaman/animist elements make their necessary and transforming return to the Tradition, *then* it will twitch into real life once more. This will be the moment when Osiris, the Horned God, will finally be given back his balls.

The Horned God was found in bull form, for example, during the Bronze and Iron Ages around the Aegean Sea, where we can find the legend of the Minotaur of Crete and see a human wearing a bull's head and horns being worshipped with dance and sacrifice. This Minotaur was held to be the sacred offspring of the Cretan queen, who appeared robed and masked as a cow, and who was mated with a foreign "bull" at regular ritual intervals. This is also tied up with the image and concept of ritual sacrifice discussed below.

And then there was Pan. There is always Pan. With his long, narrow face, small horns, and goat's legs, he is first cousin to the dancing god shown on page 78.

Pan and his ilk are directly comparable to the Aker, that "part man part beast" who guards the portals of the Underworld, and who can usher us into the mysteries of the natural realm with which it overlaps.[2]

*Two Horned Gods guarding the gate
of the Underworld*

This is true of the Horned God and his consort generally. Their concerns are with the Land (and its parallels in human consciousness) and what lies below it (and the parallels there, too). The Horned God, however he manifests himself, can be approached on a number of levels in much the same way that the simple faun, who was Pan of Arcady, came to take on levels of sophistication that the original worshippers may not have recognized or understood.

A common link between priests of different religions and cultures would have been the animal forms used in their mysteries, and the symbols which best represented their deities. They would have been able to discuss their totemic beasts in much the same way that

people today can ask: "What sort of car do you have?" —
which in itself can pass on trivial clues as to status and
self-image. Arm-bands, made of the feathers, fur or
teeth of the bird or beast in question, were symbols of
the priest's allegiance, and these later became — for
security reasons — transformed into garters which
could be hidden on the leg, under clothing.

It was only when the Romans began to conquer
Europe that we begin to pick up written records of the
gods they encountered, even though these were often
described in terms of their own state religion. Even so,
as soldiers who followed the fighting man's Cult of
Mithras (which may well have overtaken Christianity
had it made some appeal to women), they would have
seen in the local Horned Gods clear echoes of the Sacred
Bull so central to their own initiation ceremonies.
Indeed, the ritual slaughter of the Mithraic "Bull of the
Sun," in whose blood the initiates were soaked, may
well have been a direct descendant of the Osirian
slaying of the Apis Bull, which in itself was held to be an
incarnation of the Horned God, Osiris, himself.

In fact we can see within this the conceptual elements of sacrifice as "going down through the worlds,"
in a manner of speaking. First, there was the willing
sacrifice of humans. Then, when humanity outgrew
this need, it was animals. Today, in the Christian
church, we can find an expression of what might be
called vegetable sacrifice during the English Harvest
Festival, when produce is offered up on the altar. The
mineral sacrifice is part of a mystery still to come.

So, to get back to our theme, it was through the
Romans that we can begin to pick up Cernunnos.

The word itself is Latinized Celtic, found inscribed
on the altar which lay under the Christian altar of the
Cathedral of Notre Dame in Paris. The name simply

means "Horned One," or even "Old Hornie."

> The name appears in every variation throughout
> the area of Indo-European speech. The chief god of
> the Fertility Cult . . . was (and is still) known in Ire-
> land as Conall Cernac. His name is enshrined in
> both English "Cornwall" and Breton "Kerne" (the
> French "Cornouaille").[3]

It is generally held that the shrine of Cern in Paris
was "rehabilitated" by being overlaid with the new faith
of Christianity, but this was not always the case.
Sometimes places of power, which were also places of
worship, just came to the end of their useful life as far as
the original energies went. This might be compared to a
battery going flat. Rightly or wrongly, the Christianity
of the time simply recharged each place, tapping those
forces which lay beneath, but in a different way and at a
different frequency. It was not always a simple matter
of one faith obliterating another. At least, not in the
earliest days, when Christians still knew how to work
with power. The overlying of the original altar in this
case was not an instance of religious conquest and
suppression, but a sacramental act which acknowledged that which had gone before.

The same God, Cern, can be found in Brittany. This
is a region that has never regarded itself as being
French, and which is wrapped up in the figure of Saint
Cornely. This saint is an imaginary pope said to have
been martyred in 253 A.D. — a fate which is peculiarly
appropriate as far as Horned Gods are concerned. He is
the patron saint of horned beasts and he is always
depicted in church statuary and banners in the company of a bull. His name comes from the old Gaulish
word for "horn," which is a potent symbol that is

outwardly male, but inwardly female. The snake swallowing its own tail manages to convey the same concept of male and female conjoined in one body. It is perhaps because of this idea that snakes are often depicted along with Cernunnos.

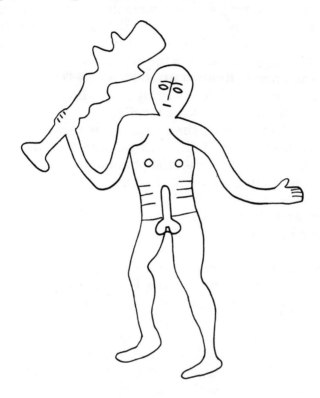

The Cerne Abbas hill carving

We can find him again on the other side of the Channel — almost directly opposite in Cerne Abbas, Dorset, where in Anglo-Saxon times a large monastic foundation grew up on the site of a shrine. Here, carved on the chalk hillside above the site, the massive club-wielding giant still rules supreme. The Christian monastery came and went, but the old God still remains, no longer horned but clearly "horny."[4]

Although the word *cerne* is invariably pronounced with a soft *c* today (thus "Sern Abbas"), it is recognized that "kern" is the older and more accurate pronunciation. However, I would go one further and suggest that it should be pronounced with the sort of rasp that should be given to the *ch* in the Scottish word *loch*, lake. It is the anemic English attempt to say "Cern" in its proper manner which has resulted in him being called "Herne," for the sake of the tonsils.

The Cerne giant, then, was once regarded as a wondrous source of fertility. Barren women had only to sit upon him — ideally on the phallus itself — in order to become fertile; although most people felt that it was more effective for a husband and wife to have full intercourse there to cure the same problem. The giant was, and is, not just a chalk carving on a hillside, but a key that could unlock fertilities within those who approached him properly. In the small enclosure above his head, known today as the Frying Pan, a maypole was said to have been erected annually for the May Day celebrations, which were in themselves descendants of those great pre-Christian feasts of Beltaine. Wherever the maypole was really erected, whether in Cerne or anywhere else, we have a superb and obvious symbol of the Earth God becoming hard for the benefit of his people. Quite literally, by means of the colored cords radiating from the tip of the pole, and onto which the dancers held, the people bound themselves to him.

Our old friend Geb would have been at home in Cerne Abbas, where the erect giant can still be seen sprawled across the earth below the arching sky.

One way or another, he is ...

So in various ways and for various reasons the Horned God's worship co-existed with Christianity long enough to reach that era when details of his priesthood began to be written down; even though this was invariably done from a jaundiced viewpoint, and from one in which any God other than Jesus or Jehovah was necessarily the very manifestation of Darkness. A few examples have survived, however, and these are worth looking at.

There was Suibhne (Sweeney) Gelt, King of the Dal Araidhe in Northern Ireland, who went mad after the major battle of Magh Rath in 642 A.D. He then wandered desolate regions, often showing evidence of supernatural powers. These included the ability to ride upon a fawn and exert control over the wild stags of his bleak world. Indeed, he had a herd of stags which he used to pull ploughs — a hint of the old deities of agriculture working under the aegis of the Stag God. Suibhne Gelt was so identified with stags, in fact, that he was emphatically described as being a herbivore, or more poetically a "tongue of the wild land," made to crawl among cresses.

Then comes the Black Man, from the *Romance of Owain,* who was:

> ...as large as two ordinary men; he has but one foot, and one eye in the middle of his forehead. And he has a club of iron, and certainly there are no two men in the world who could bear that club. And he is no handsome man, but on the contrary exceedingly ugly; and he is the ranger of the wood. And you will see a thousand wild animals grazing around him.[5]

As Owain later said, with awe, the animals "bowed

their heads, and did him homage as their Lord." The term "ranger of the wood," and his general role as something of a guardian and protector, points to the fact that specific areas, such as woods, mountains, lakes, and so on, very often have entities associated with them which, for lack of a better term, we might simply describe as "lesser gods." At least that is how they would have been regarded in earlier times. Thus a particular area, and every creature living within it, would fall under the aegis of something or someone akin to Owain's extraordinary Black Man. Once, on a bitter and pure winter's day in Wisconsin, I made a tenuous and delightful contact with a young and half-awake entity that was entirely linked to a large pond, only waiting for the long days of the sun to come around again. But the Black Man in Owain's adventures was rather more than this. In fact, his blackness is a pure Osirian symbol — a reference to the silt, which covered his body when Isis first recovered it from the Nile — silt which in itself is a symbol replete with fertile associations. But it is in the single eye that we are made to consider him more carefully. Through that, we are thrown far beyond the more immediate and popular associations with the Cyclops of Greek mythology, and we find ourselves standing before the Heliopolitan mythology once more.

In that extraordinary battle which Horus had with Set, and which lasted as long as most mortals' lives, the hawk-god had his eye plucked out. This eye was given to Osiris by his son as a symbol of the confirmation of the new regime — the new order which had been established by his accession. The eye which remained was the Sun, and the one he lost was, in essence, the Moon. All of which is an indication of the sort of change in evolutionary consciousness we will discuss in due course.

This hearkens quite neatly on toward Norse mythology and the supreme figure of Odin. He gained his wisdom from beneath the famous ash tree, Yggdrasil, whose roots link the Underworld with the Heaven-World and which conceal an eagle, a squirrel, and four stags. Under these roots lay Mimir's Well. The wisdom of Mimir was only exchanged for the sacrifice of Odin's eye. And Odin, so the prophecies go, will one day be swallowed by the great wolf Fenris, who is none other than our friend Anubis again, in Northern guise.

This single-eye motif, then, is not one of deformity, but of knowledge. It is invariably linked with the concept of dominion over natural realms. The other eye, that which is lost or "given," still exists within the Otherworld. There is an allusive (and elusive) reference here to the old Scottish Highland idea of a person having "Two Sights"— one of the natural world and one of the realm beyond. But these single-eyed figures often come to us in dreams of a specific and highly peculiar kind. Most dreams — the vast bulk of them — are little more than the water dripping down an overflow pipe. We can simply let them drain away. But we do occasionally get those which are meant to "awaken" us.

These cyclopean dream-figures often occur during those times in a person's life when he or she is coming more surely under the shadow of the Horned God and his Lady. They might be regarded as signs of the awakening of particular brain-cells, and do not necessarily appear in our dreams to pass on specific information.

But these myths of Black Men and stag-herders apart, the highwater mark of Horned God descriptions

Yggdrasill, the World Tree of the Edda
From Finnur Magnusson's edition of the Elder Edda, 18th century

is surely to be found in the *Vita Merlini* of Geoffrey of Monmouth, issued in 1150 A.D.

The Merlin of this book is far more primitive though no less appealing than the smooth and courtly figure so enduringly presented in the more popular Arthurian romances. Here he is shown as a true Lord of Stags, living alone in the woods with his favorite companions of the pig and the wolf. The deer, naturally, obey him. He wears an antlered helmet. He eats as the deer eat. He has a wife/sister Gwendoloena. For a period of his life he was said to have gone mad and retreated into the wilderness, uttering prophecies about the world to come.

Indeed, in one way or one level or another, this is something that happens to us all at some stage in our lives. Joseph Campbell described the three phases as being separation, initiation, and return. The separation comes to us in the course of everyday life when, for reasons that are apparently beyond our control, our worlds fall apart, there is loneliness, savagery, and wilderness within us and around us; we have moods and experience feelings of such intensity and darkness that, in later years, we can only describe it as having gone through a kind of madness. This is the phase of Osiris Torn and Scattered, and it is the time of Merlin disintegrating into the forest. It is only later that we find our own initiations, and learn to begin again armed with the sudden (and blessedly temporary) conviction that we do now begin to understand some of the darker sides of life and can make our own predictions and interpolations accordingly.

This, of course, is an exceedingly mundane version of Merlin's experience, but one that is no less valid than others.

Now there are, necessarily, many Merlins, and many

nations claiming him for their own. Nikolai Tolstoy, in
his *The Quest for Merlin,* makes a brilliant case for his
origins to be found on the Hart Fell, near the present-
day town of Moffat, on the Scottish Border. To him
Merlin was:

> ...the horned deity who watched over men and
> beasts, and received the souls of the departed into
> his habitation in the sky. He wore an antlered
> helm (probably deerskins as well), and in some de-
> gree acted out the part of the stag itself. His station
> was by a sacred spring on the edge of a mountain in
> the centre of the Caledonian Forest... A sacred ap-
> ple tree or orchard grew nearby, and [he] was at-
> tended by animal familiars in the form of a pig and
> a wolf. The whole are of the mountain was re-
> garded with awe and fear...[6]

But whether Merlin has the cervine qualities of
Geoffrey of Monmouth's account, or the more political,
King-making functions described by Thomas Malory
and Robert de Boron, the Burgundian poet who also
wrote about Joseph of Arimathea, his essential character remains the same — strong and often acid, roguish,
insightful, capable of great flashes of anger and raw,
truly magical power. But above all he is concerned for
the people whose destinies he often guided.

The very name Merlin, of course, refers to "a little
bird," the name given to a small European falcon. In the
present-day sport of falconry, which has even under-
gone a minor revival in recent times, the different sorts
of hawks and their ideal human partners are still to be
found listed as they were centuries before: a gerfalcon is
for a king, a peregrine for an earl, a goshawk for a
yeoman, sparrow-hawk for a priest, kestrel for a knave
— and a merlin for a lady.

Another figure relating to our present theme is that of Lailoken, who first appeared in the 12th century *Life of St. Kentigern,* the patron saint of Glasgow. Lailoken was described as a madman who was kept at the court of King Rhydderch, rather like a resident shaman who often made startling prophecies. He had been driven mad during a battle fought along the banks of the River Liddel. In this battle, a host of warriors — dead souls — had appeared in the sky and accused Lailoken of having been responsible for all the slaughter. Tormented and driven by the voices within himself, he ran off into the forest where (like Suibhne Gelt, and for the same reasons) he lived the naked life of a wild man. In these tales, he is expressly identified with Merlin. Textual evidence also links him with the Myrddin of Welsh poetry, who is also unmistakably the Merlin of Geoffrey of Monmouth.

In all cases, we come across the same themes of wilderness and/or wasteland, control of beasts, the dissolution of the personality, and the ability to "see" beyond this world. Looming over all these is the great bellowing image of the stag. In varying ways, all of these ideas are born along by stags and linked with the concept of kings and kingship.

And then there is Gwyn ap Nudd, "Light, Son of Darkness," of whom William G. Gray makes the comment:

> Actually "Light, son of Darkness" signifies the old FIAT LUX, or the well-known Yang-Yin. It's just the old Celtic name for a Power of Eternal Alternation . . . Almost anything could be expected of him. As Day came out of Night, Life came out of Death, Yes came out of No, and so creation continued . . . In point of fact the whole damn thing developed out

of what we now call shamanism. A sort of Nature Religion which arose from peoples personal experiences and reactions with Nature itself. This resulted in a response from specific humans causing a character-change that seemed to "set them apart" from their ordinary fellows and "make them special" so that they were considered to be priests or at least have what we now call Psi-powers, or uncommon faculties such as telepathy, clairvoyance, and possibly healing. Eventually it became noticed that this was becoming hereditary within familial lines. Once the connections had time to build up definite establishments and power-structures began . . . In time standard ceremonials were being handed down from one generation to another down the centuries, but at the back of everything the old spontaneous experience persisted . . . In other words those who had "attained" priesthood for several lives eventually got born with the knowledge and experience *in their genes already* so that the priesthood became an hereditary function . . . However the ancestral memories of the early experiences have always been there, and humans have called them out in hopes of reviving the old links with ancient times so that it may be said in the old words of Adam: "My priesthood and my gift of prophecy shall He restore to me etc. . . ." when speaking of the coming crucifixion.[7]

Make links with Gwyn, awaken impulses within the genes, and he will restore our potentials as priests and priestesses. Through him, we can initiate ourselves. Through his ancient vision, we can attempt to create new futures.

Like the very best of Horned Gods, not much is known about Gwyn. Students of popular folklore describe him as the Welsh Lord of the Fairies, which to the modern ear tends to give him simpering, tinkling, "wimpish" qualities. However, the modern idea of fairies as diminutive creatures is a condition somewhat akin to looking down the wrong end of a mytho-historical telescope. Fairies, fees, or fays was the common name for the original inhabitants of Europe.

> The fairies, then, were the descendants of the early people who inhabited northern Europe; they were pastoral but not nomad, they lived in the unforested parts of the country where there was good pasturage for their cattle, and they used stone in the Neolithic period and metal in the Bronze Age for their tools and weapons ... Undoubtedly as civilisation advanced and more land came under cultivation the fairy people must have mingled more and more with the settled population, till many of them entered the villages and became indistinguishable from the "mortals."[8]

They were indeed small in stature compared to the later invaders — probably no more than five feet tall at best; but they certainly did not live in buttercups or tulips! In fact, they lived in circular huts which were sunk into the ground to a depth of two or three feet. The roofs of these huts were supported by a central pole and wooden frame, the entire structure then covered in turf and bracken and shrubs, so that they looked like mounds, or small hills. These were the People of the Hills — the fairies and the witches. These are the descendants of those cave-dwellers who worshipped the Stag God in the Artiege, and who danced to the mystic tune of that God from Le Fourneau du Diable. Gwyn ap Nudd is his title on the British Isle, and we can give him the personal name of Herne. Merlin, Lailoken, Suibhne Gelt, and all the rest were his priests.

The fays — let us call them that — were not, however, some distant and doomed race that can mean no more to us than some paleolithic graffiti and a few myths. The fays no longer exist because they intermarried with those races that came afterward. The fays are to be found within our furthest ancestors, There is fay blood in all of us. They, and their pantheons — simple though they were — are part of our genetic structure.

Soon, we will learn to meet up with them.

Gwyn ap Nudd has two main associations which might seem trivial in themselves, but which can lead us into some extraordinarily vast areas for research. The first association is with Glastonbury Tor, and the second is with the Wild Hunt.

The Tor, which simply means "hill," has a reputation in England for power and sanctity which other nationalities find hard to understand. It is regarded as the holy place in the British Isles, certainly, and possibly the rest of the world as a whole — if its most ardent admirers are to be believed. This may or may not be true. Certainly there is a staggering accretion of legends connected with the Tor and the town which have gathered like moths to the light.

There are many who believe that under the waters of a spring and the slopes of the Tor, which is topped by a 14th-century church tower, Joseph of Arimathea buried what became known as the Holy Grail. They also believe that when, on a nearby hill, he thrust his thorn staff into the ground, it took root to produce the distinctive Glastonbury winter-flowering thorn-tree. Still further, they believe that he built a church of wattle and daub on the site where the ruins of the great abbey now stand and that there he made the first conversions to Christianity in Britain. It has long been an English conceit that Joseph, as a merchant who traded in tin, made regular trips to the mines in the nearby Mendip Hills and brought his nephew, Jesus, with him on at least one occasion.

If this was so, then, at the time when they made the voyage, the town itself would have been an island in the middle of marshes and lakes. A shallow sea would, at flood tides, lap its way some 20 miles inland to the very foot of the Tor itself.

In about 688 A.D., King Ine of Wessex gave Glastonbury a monastery which was regarded as the most beautiful in the land. A tomb can still be seen within the grounds which the monks claimed to have been that of Arthur, although some folk secretly whispered that it was that of Gwyn. Other legends have it that Arthur and his knights are sleeping below the Tor, like Osiris, waiting for the moment when they will be needed to "save the land" once more.

Geoffrey Ashe, the formidable Arthurian scholar, makes a potent case for the Tor being the wondrous temple described by Roman historians as the principal focus for the mysteries in Britain. In fact, the whole area has been seen as ringed by a zodiac formed by the natural features of the land — the heavens brought down and sealed within the Earth.

So it is here, in a small and otherwise unremarkable town which specializes in sheepskin products and a livestock market, that the supreme examples of the Pagan and Christian Mysteries co-exist and indeed thrive. Only those cafes displaying signs saying "No Hippies" give any indication that the conjunction has, occasionally, caused tensions of a different and purely mundane kind.

Glastonbury, in the hearts of many, is the true power-center of Britain: like the grail/cauldron/crystal ball, all things can be found within it if you know how and when to look. It may be a small town in Somerset to the earthly eye, but, to the visionary, it is a gateway to Avalon.

According to occultists, there is a Gate atop the Tor which leads to the Otherworld/ Underworld. It is here that Gwyn can be found and here that we can find our ways back to the thesis of the first chapter. Here the Horned God can be found guarding the Moon Gate behind which lie dragons, dead souls and the infinite sources of life itself. We are back to the concept of Osiris dwelling in the Tuat, but coming to the Gate at daily intervals to offer us entry. These are the Gods of Life and also of Death, as these qualities are seen as different sides of the same door.

It has always been argued by the occultist that peoples of previous ages, such as the fays, had faculties that have since atrophied in modern humanity. It is implied that the loss of these faculties was something of a minor Fall from a more blessed state.

But that was not quite the case. These faculites certainly existed — and exist today. They can awaken with surprising ease when people find themselves living in isolated places for long periods of time. Silence shows that it has sensual, living qualities of its own, and that it is far more than simply an absence of noise. Isolation proves to be anything but seclusion. Those faculties that we imagined had been lost to the aeons come creeping out like timid mice. The Two Sights, and similar faculties, begin to open once more.

But, as Julian Jaynes has shown in his book, *The Origin of Consciousness in the Breakdown of the Bicameral Mind,* this can be seen more accurately, perhaps, as a description of the way humanity's mode of thinking changed from being right-brain dominated to find itself functioning essentially through the left hemisphere.

In crude and simple terms (the best kind there are), the left brain deals with intellect, analysis, linear thinking, cause-and-effect, mechanical time — all qualities that we can conveniently describe as Solar, and which relate to the Qabalistic sphere of Chokmah.

In contrast, the right brain is concerned with intuition, gestalt, nonlinear thinking, synchronicity, and timelessness, which we might regard as being Lunar, and linked with the sphere of Binah.

As Jaynes asserts, from a non-occult viewpoint, tribal members would feel themselves to be part of a common consciousness. They would be aware of the prescence of the departed and would be able to function collectively, as certain groupings within the animal and bird world so obviously do. The voice cf their consciences would resonate in their mental ears with the voices of their dead fathers, or dead kings. Best of all, their dead kings.

> Osiris . . . was the hallucinated voice of a dead king whose admonitions could still carry weight. And since he could still be heard [via right-brain consciousness], there is no paradox in the fact that the body from which the voice came should be mummified, with all the equipment of the tomb providing life's necessities . . . There was no mysterious power that emanated from him; simply his remembered voice which appeared in hallucination to those who had known him and which could admonish or suggest even as it had before he stopped moving and breathing.[9]

The principle is correct, no doubt about it. Jaynes, however, does not take into account the possibility that such inner voices, heard via the right-brain functions, could often be *exactly what they seem*. In any case the whole scheme must be counterbalanced by those researchers who turn the flow of consciousness around 90 degrees, in a sense, and attribute these same qualities to the functions of the cerebrum and cerebellum instead.

It is interesting to note that, when the occultist Dion Fortune described the consciousness of the Atlantean commoner, she noted, rather disparagingly, that they had little more intelligence than dogs. Today, she might well ascribe those dog-like characteristics to the tight, tribal collective of right-brain consciousness, as seen from afar by a 20th century visionary.

The point is that, with this right-brain consciousness, there was an absolute certainty that man did survive after death. However they expressed this survival in their religious systems, death, as an experience, was completely devoid of the terrors that it has for us today. It was not a matter of faith. It is not a matter of holding up some desperately-held belief system as a shield against the nightmare . . . the reality of the Otherworld and each person's survival there was part of everyday experience.

The Gods of the Old Religions, if we may call them that, contained within themselves Life and Death, Light and Darkness, Giving and Taking, Male and Female, Outer and Inner. They balanced; they were one. There was no exaltation of one at the expense of the other. So must the Tor balance the Abbey, the Pagan with the Christian, the hill with the valley. Taking up a crude but immediate analogy: Society today is rather like a branch plucked from a tree, split part way down its length and pulled apart. The tensions at the end of the split, where the whole branch begins, are enormous. As the outward pressure on the split prongs continues, disaster becomes immanent. The branch is likely to burst apart entirely. Society, shaped liked the divining rods used by the old-fashioned dowsers, quivers before our astonished gaze. So the pressure must be relaxed, the split healed, Life and Death seen to channel the same saps, and the branch placed carefully into the earth in the hope that it might flower once again.

The Glastonbury region is an image of the universe, and therefore of Humanity. We can find anything we want there — Holy Grails, saints, once and future kings, mystic caverns, ley-lines. But we have to find them in ourselves first. We are all Isles of Glass set within shallow seas. "Behind the smiling mirror, and Behind the smiling moon, Follow, Follow . . ." as T. S. Eliot said.

Balance is needed. Between the hemispheres of the brain, the left and the right, the outward and inward. Gwyn ap Nudd is one of those gods who can show us precisely where the dividing line is, and how to make use of it. What he does not want — not these days — is our worship. We need the gods and the gods need us. We need the gods to teach us things; they need us to experience. The flow is entirely mutual and two-way. This is neither heresy, hubris, nor megalomania, but a way forward into a New Age. The old initiatic cry: "There is no part of me which is not also part of the Gods!" can now be inverted to read: "There is no part of the Gods which can not be found in me." So Gwyn can be as easily contacted by means of a solitary lighted candle in a small apartment in the heart of an American city as he can upon the windswept heights of Glastonbury Tor. It all has to do with heart, and with intention.

Ultimately, we will show how Gwyn is concerned with both the spirit of place and the place of spirit, and deal with the concept of the land as a living, knowing entity. Neither of them want our worship, but they do want our *work*. The Earth in particular is a battered, abused, and raped woman. Such a woman does not want to be worshipped — she wants help, healing, and understanding. The time for crude worship is past.

So Gwyn rises to us in dreams and visions. He can bring us those salves and unguents which can help heal the bruises and breaks within the world and within ourselves. We could do worse than become his priests and priestesses for a while, knowing that one day we will ride at his back, with the Wild Hunt — when our own earthly cares have been left far behind ... The Wild Hunt is one of those themes which has left its mark in European folklore without anyone being particularly clear as to its true nature. At one time, it was seen in the skies as often as UFOs are today, and it provoked the same kind of excitement and awe. Its first recorded appearance in England was at Peterborough in Lincolnshire in the year 1127:

> these hunters were black, and huge and ugly, and they rode on black horses and deer. They were seen in the very deer-park of the town of Peterborough ... and the monks heard the blasts of the horns which they blew in the night.[10]

These Hunts, sometimes in the sky and sometimes through the forest rides, were seen all over Europe. In the German tradition, it is a spectral hunter with a pack of dogs, particularly associated with the Black Forest. In France, *Le Grand Veneur* courses through Fontainebleu Forest; in Britain, the honors are shared between Herne, of Windsor Forest, and Gwyn himself; while it is Odin, or Woden, who leads the spectral company through more northerly climes. In some cases, the huntsmen themselves were held to be the souls of pagan corpses, forever condemned to pursue a mystic hart across the darkling worlds. In others, they were the souls of dead warriors.

There is something almost touching about the former: a vision, perhaps, of medieval man's conscience allowing him a mystic glimpse of those lost parts of himself coursing through the stars in pursuit of a rapidly vanishing god — the true god of the land of his heart, if he were to face it.

Herne, the Hunter

So it was Herne, from his home in the royal forest of Windsor, who led the Hunt among the English in later centuries, while the Celts, with their older subconscious memories, referred to him as Gwyn ap Nudd, and taught that he gathered up dead souls and carried them to his realm via that Gate within the Hill of Vision, or Glastonbury Tor. If he was ever seen accompanied by his Hounds of Hell, like the *bean-sidhe* (banshees) of Irish myth, it was a sure sign that mortals witnessing the vision were themselves about to die. In time, in more ways than one, people did not look at all. In time, in more ways than one, people were no longer able to see.

Several modern magicians have had the experience of being denied access to the Tor — and other holy hills — as if by an inner command from an external source. A command which they knew they must not, could not, deny. In each case the reason, if that is the appropriate term, was that the "Hosting of the *Sidhe*" was in progress at the summit. This is a compartively benign but no less potent version of the Wild Hunt, as the *Sidhe* (shee) are the faery race of Ireland. We have also already mentioned those mysterious conglomerations of lights frequently seen today emanating from and returning back into such places. Frequently, all of these have been lumped together under the heading of UFO phenomena. While it would be ridiculous to reject entirely the notion that we are being visited from the stars, the truth about many of these lights is more closely related to the "aliveness" of certan places within the landscape. It is particularly *hills* that come alive in discernible ways. Watching these emanations from the hill of your choice is like watching neurons firing in the brain. It is the consciousness of the hill that we see in dynamic action. Because we become linked to this particular hill in a magical relationship, we are also watching our own neurons firing. In a way, these apparently intelligent lights *are* from beyond this world. They are from the most distant future and the remotest past, for they are expressions of our most ancient genetic consciousness.

All this will be discussed again in due course, but we must get back to the inevitable question: "*What* is being pursued by the Hunt?" In that first recorded vision from Peterborough the answer is already clear: a wounded hart. But although there is also, often, the confident answer "dead souls," in too many of the other sightings the spectral horsemen are involved in more of a Wild Ride, a frenzied gallop behind their leader. Can this have any relevance to us here on earth, in the 20th Century, with all our 20th Century concerns?

A partial answer can be found in Mediterranean sources. For example, this can be seen in the story of Actaeon, who happened to see the Goddess Artemis (known as Diana to the Romans) bathing naked. Artemis, who possessed a magical silver bow, hunted Actaeon down with her hounds, transformed him into a stag, and killed him with her bow. According to Robert Graves *(The White Goddess)*, Actaeon was: "... a sacred king of the pre-Hellenic stag cult, torn to pieces at the end of his reign of 50 months ..."

We might speculate from this that the horned figure who leads the Hunt across the lightning-flecked sky is *himself* the object of pursuit in an echo of the Cult of the Sacred King. The hunter, as the saying goes, becomes the hunted. So there is Actaeon, turned into a stag and torn to pieces. There is Osiris, the Horned God, torn to pieces by Set and his many animal-like companions. And there is an oblique crosslinking between Osiris and the Hunter through the association of the Egyptian god with the constellation of Orion. The latter was a giant hunter, noted for his beauty, who was blinded by Enopian, and finally slain by Diana (known as Artemis to the Greeks).

We can indeed witness this Wild Hunt on many levels, both magical and mundane, and one as important as the other. The Hunt is integral to atmospheric disturbances — storm, lightning, and high wind — with the spectral company part and parcel of the turbulence. It is said that such storms often accompany great souls entering or leaving the world. This is especially true when the soul concerned — consciously or otherwise — was or is about to be linked with the land in some shamanic sense.

Anyone who rises to any prominence, in any profession or group, invariably becomes aware of the hounds and jackals that slowly start to gather behind him. Among modern celebrities, particularly Anglo-American political figures, this is especially noticeable. It is a curious comment upon, and perhaps indictment of, our times that whereas ancient kings and leaders had to prove their fitness for office by virtue of virility and fertility, nowadays the dogs of the media sniff over their trails through life for the slightest sign of sexual transgression. The French, who at least in this area have wisdom, can never understand why British and American politicians feel honor-bound to resign — or are *hounded* into resigning — whenever they are caught in some (invariably minor) transgression, often from the remote past. But this was always going to be an end result of the "sterility cult" created by dominant aspects of the Christian church. Sexual naughtiness among celebrities apart, aspects of this experience are fundamental to the workaday world, too. The more we attain as individuals, the more our inner fertilities find singular expressions that can push us out beyond the pack, the more likely it becomes that the pack will want to rip us apart. This is not paranoia, or shouldn't be. It is more simply a knowledge that we live out rituals in our lives which, however crude and corrupted they are, still can help us link with energies from the oldest times.

All of this takes us back to that Moon Gate which lies between the Human and the Natural Worlds, and is guarded by that Horned God who is part man, part beast, and who can show us the way to the oldest parts of ourselves. If, in the historical sense, his worship became as dismembered as he regularly was, then we can find it echoed today within spiritualist and Wiccan circles.

At first glance, this seems absurd, but they are in fact two parts of one formidable equation. Many spiritualists today are linked by previous existences in which they functioned, quite simply, as witches. Unfortunately, the spiritualist movement itself is too often limited by its rather brittle and apparently shallow dogma, and shaded over by the infernally Christian nature of its approach. It is invariably (and unfairly) seen as the refuge of the weak, simple, and elderly. On the other hand, as far as Wicca goes, there are very few witches around today who have one tenth of the extraordinary talents and healing abilities the best spiritualist mediums have. They know a great deal about occult philosophies, and have entirely laudable "green" attitudes, but they are too often sadly lacking in any real power.

If the two were able to combine, somehow, so that we could get a spiritualist movement with passionate Nature links (in the magical sense), and which was not afraid of sex, or else a witch with the full and deep complement of spiritualist powers, then we would have a potent mix indeed. We would have a shamanic figure ripe to wear the crown of a near-forgotten god.

In a sense, both spiritualism and Witchcraft today lie scattered at either side of the Moon Gate as fragments of a once cohesive power. They are the broken halves of a crown — the crown itself being a stylized version of the stag's helm or similar ritual adornment.

Someday this crown *will* be retrieved and restored. An American woman will appear who will be a child of Coyote (who is really Anubis letting his hair down, so to speak). She will have a vision of a bear, an open mouth, an expanse of cold, dark water, and a place of glittering sharpness. In time, she will join these two traditions together and take us all a little further through that Gate.

Apart from the Horned God pure and simple, there are other figures from history and legend who have become imbued with that green light that shines from within him. Any figure with strong Earth or Water connections is ripe for investiture as a priest of the Horned God.

Robin Hood is the classic example. In fact, the name Robin (meaning "Bright Flame") was often ascribed to the god of those witches who came up against their Christian inquisitors. Witches in Somerset claimed that their god was called up simply by calling the name Robin three times. A simple enough method, but one which is entirely effective today, as we shall see.

Robin of the Hood may well be a reference to those helmets which the priests wore, and which were necessarily large enough to support the horns of whatever deity they used. Or it may be that, with the great linguistic changes that occurred in this medieval period, the term Robin of the Wood became pronounced Robin 'Ood — which still later linguistic changes rationalized and modernised as Robin Hood. (In England, the stress is on the third syllable of the name rather than on the first, as in the American pronunciation.)

Robin of the Hood and/or Robin of the Wood would be the local deity whose energies were mediated by the appropriate priest and priestess.

Of course, the name "Bright Flame" is one that can make sparks fly within the imagination of any romantically inclined magician — the bright flame, the Light

Robin Goodfellow, c. 1628

from Darkness, the shining spirit of the woods. There are links, too, between Robin Hood/Wood and the intriguing figure of Robin Goodfellow, the guiding spirit of more than one coven, who was described as a powerful, horned, and bearded man, yet one who was pure and virile goat from the waist down — even to the cloven hooves. He carried a witches broom over one shoulder, a wooden phallus of sorts in his right hand, and had a hunting horn slung over his other shoulder. He was an early 17th century answer to the Great God Pan, as far as some contemporary academics were concerned, but they were always missing the real truth about him.

Nevertheless Pan, Cheiron, the Aker, and all those many entities from Mediterranean myth systems which are part human and part beast can be found at the same place within our consciousness as Gwyn, waiting in that timeless manner of theirs for us to make the necessary links.

Of course, it was easier to make these links in previous Ages, for reasons already given. In those Ages, communities were isolated in ways and to degrees that we can not easily appreciate today. Each community had its own family of invisible creatures which bonded with them, and with whom they worked on outer and inner levels. There was indeed a complete unity between these levels. There was no difference. But the onus of accurate and detailed communication was laid at the door of that shamanic figure who later came to be described as a witch. The ability to work in this way came to be something of a family trait. Peculiar talents were passed on through the genes from one generation to another, kept within the ranks of specific families, and this only began to diminish when the communities themselves began to be fragmented by the changeing times.

In an oblique reference to this there is an extraordinary piece of folk-memory preserved in John Michell's *Megalithomania:*

> [At Callanish on the Isle of Lewis] the old people still held certain families in special respect and esteem as "belonging to the Stones" ... The old man also told him that when the sun rose on Midsummer morning "Something" came to the Stones, walking down the great avenue heralded by the cuckoo's call. He had described the "Something" by a word [which] was probably pre-Gaelic, and from

from a root common to the British group of languages. It meant, they thought, the Shining, or
Pure, or White one . . . and had probably been the
epithet of a god.[11]

These are the People of the Stones who are just as
involved with the "Bright Flame" as the People of the
Wood, or Hood. In both cases they know that the land is
alive, and that the spirit(s) behind their own localized
portion of it had an interest in working with them, and
for them, if they could just understand the spirit
properly.

In another Element, too, there is the figure of Sir
Francis Drake, whom the Spaniards called El Draco, or
the Dragon — which is what his name actually means.
An extraordinary man who explored vast areas of a
hitherto unsuspected world, he became widely regarded after his death as having been larger than life.
He is thought to have had definite magical powers, and
his drum is said to beat even today when England is in
peril. Many people through the centuries have claimed
to have heard this beat, which might be likened to the
heart beat of the nation itself. His former manor,
Combe Sydenham in Devon, resonates with some
peculiar energies. But best of all, as a proof of identity,
local legends after his death coincidently described him
as the foremost rider in the Wild Hunt.

Robin of the Wood claimed the Earth and the Trees
for his domain; Sir Francis Drake had the Sea and its
waves. Under the masks, both men were the same.

Any hero figure closely associated with the Elements
can be used to crack open the Moon Gate even if these
figures a) never existed or b) existed, but in reality had
no interest in any spiritual matters. Frontiersmen
provide a fine example for the American magician —

men who lived on the edge of Nature and who attracted tales and taller tales about their deeds . . . Daniel Boone, Davy Crockett, Kit Carson — they can all be used. Or rather, their *images* can be used, which is not quite the same thing. If obscure Chancellors from obscure periods in British history can be used by the followers of Dion Fortune to bring through material and experience of unquestionable value,[12] and if the witches' contacts with Robin of the Woods can do similar things, then there can be nothing absurd about expecting that one day the King of the Wild Frontier might come to do the same for his own people.

In literary terms, we also have the reality of the Gypsy and the image of the gamekeeper to provide us with some further lore. Some believe the Gypsies to be remnants of a "'gyptian" tribe which made the great migration from their homeland along the Nile, bearing arcane knowledge with them. Regardless of the truth of the Gypsies — whether they are decayed Egyptian stock or an Indic people speaking the Indo-European language of Romany or remnants of the fays, or all three — they are people who live outside society, closer to Nature than the rest of us. They are generally credited with hereditary faculties such as the Two Sights, which often made them objects of fear. On another continent entirely, the American Indians have exactly the same role and position, although they seem to have retained their mysteries in a far more cohesive and enduring manner. Indeed, it can be argued that they, more than any other racial group, contain the secrets of the next Age.

So, clearly, the Moon Gate is a crowded place. Or it would be, rather, if we continued to lok at it with a universal eye. Soon, we will learn to take a gentle flail to all these images — for at the moment that is all they

are, empty images — and drive away all that do not
concern us, flicking at them as Pharaoh must once have
flicked at the desert flies. Once that is done, we will be
left with our two originals, the Horned God and the
Horned Goddess, however we choose to name them. We
will learn to pick up their messages at whatever
frequencies they broadcast upon.

But before we can do that we must tie up some loose
ends, and bring the main themes of the book full circle.
We must look at the Cult of the Sacred Kings and the
Sacrificed Gods, and learn how even in these obscure
realities from the darkest ages of world history, a
message for the brightest futures can still be found.

Notes

[1]Graham Webster, *The British Celts and their Gods under Rome.* (London: Batsford, 1986).

[2]The magician C. R. F. Seymour commented "... these 'conductors of the dead' are also in many cases the instigators of the teachings of the Mysteries. Their role of 'Walker of Two Worlds' made them the guardian of neophyte and initiate alike ..."

[3]Michael Harrison, *The Roots of Witchcraft* (London: Muller, 1973), p. 84.

[4]And he can be found in Cern, in Switzerland, in a completely different way, where the multi-national research physicists accelerate pencil-sized beams of sub-atomic electrons and positrons to all but the speed of light in opposite directions around a 16-mile circular tunnel. Those particles, crashing together, produce energy of the intensity matched only in the first millisecond of the original Big Bang which created the universe in the first place.

[5]Quoted by Nikolai Tolstoy in *The Quest for Merlin,* Hutchinson.

[6]*Ibid.,* p. 86.

[7]Personal correspondence.

[8]Margaret Murray, *The God of the Witches* (London: Oxford University Press, 1953), pp. 52-53.

[9]Julian Jaynes, *The Origin of Consciousness in the Breakdown of the Bicameral Mind.* (Boston: Houghton Mifflin Co., 1976), p. 187.

[10]*The Anglo-Saxon Chronicle,* quoted by Tolstoy, *op. cit.*

[11]John Michell, *Megalithomania.* (London: Thames and Hudson, 1982), pp. 102-103

[12]See Alan Richardson and Geoff Hughes, *Ancient Magicks for a New Age.* (St. Paul, MN: Llewellyn, 1989).

And the Places of Sacrifice

In the realm of the Celts there were four great occasions when the veil between the worlds was thinner than usual, and when it became easier to pass through. These were on the feast-days of Candlemas, on February 2nd; of Beltaine, on May 1st; Lammas, on August 1st; and Samhain, November 1st. In truth, however, the actual calendrical date was far less important than the night of the nearest full moon. Of all the occasions, Samhain was in many ways the most striking. This was the beginning of the *Blotmonath,* the Bloodmonth, when the cattle and other livestock (known as quick-goods) were slaughtered and preserved to last the communities throughout the incoming winter. Samhain was also when the ancestors, the honorable spirits of the dead, were prone to gather in a yearly communion of loved ones, both living or long since gone.

It was in these months that Kings were sacrificed, or ritually slain. Specifically, it was in the Bloodmonth that Camelot came to an end, when a bright young King shed his blood upon the land to release the best of impulses in those people who adored him.

Once, in a life beyond this one, far removed from my present days, upon a high hill in Wiltshire, I received the news of that death while still in the body of a boy fretting on the edge of puberty within a cold and windswept world. It is the clearest of all my "far memories" in many ways: I was looking over a scrubbed wooden counter on which stood some brightly colored jars and bottles, just tall enough to rest my chin on the ridges of the wood made smooth by the countless hands and elbows which rested upon it; the smell of cooking in some primitive apparatus; the smell of the grease and the fat which attended the art. The stink of smoke was on everyone's clothes, and a portly woman with a dark blue apron saying in a guttural voice: "Aye, he's deed ... Ah'm tellin' ye he's deed!" The voices around, on my side of the counter, muttered disbelief, the faces bearing a kind of exultant sorrow at hearing such staggering news. *Ner, Ner,* I thought. *Nivver ... Nivver in this weorld.*

But this is not, in the reincarnational sense at least, a past life that I am recalling, but the clearest and purest memory of having been in Allington's fish and chip shop, in my home town in the northeast of England, as I heard from the astonished lady with the battered cod the astonishing news that President Kennedy had been assassinated, It was a death whose reverberations spread across the world and rippled through us all, one of those moments that no one ever forgets. That, after all, is what the death of Sacred Kings is all about.

Now, absurd as it may seem at first, Kennedy, whose name means "The Helmeted Chief," *can* be seen as another in the long line of Sacred Kings, even if the patterns of his "kingship" had become distorted. There was the ability to talk easily to and identify with the common man, even if his own family were far removed from their level in terms of wealth and status. There was the family itself, perceived as being both charmed and cursed, as "special" families inevitably are. There was his extraordinary sexual appetite which was like a wry interpretation of the Fertility God's true function. There was that seductive and indefinable aura of his which was only exceeded by that possessed by his wife Jackie. She was, if not a "white shadow" in the true sense of the term, at least a gleaming aspect of his presidency in other ways. There was even the name "Camelot," bestowed upon his administration by the media because of the innate glitter that seemed to shine from within its nature. And there was the death itself, before the eyes of the world, which had been foretold, warned against, and indeed fully expected among some pundits. There were the staggering parallels with Lincoln's death, which prompted some to drag up karmic theories. Then there was the springing-up of the mysteries — the conspiracy theories, the cover-ups — all the rough and muffled echoes of those mysteries which must surround the death of any Sacrificial King. And then there came the rumors about his after-death state (these most significant of all), which insisted that Kennedy was not dead but paralyzed, and that at some time — some future moment of national peril — their "Helmeted Chief" would be wheeled out to inspire America with hope and courage anew.

All this may seem absurd or impossible. Yet, on some levels, it is infinitely true.

Kennedy was by no means the only American hero to fit into these parameters. Walt Disney's body was supposedly preserved in cryogenic tanks (like Merlin in his crystal cave) until the era when science could revive him. Jim Morrison of the Doors rock group was never really buried in Paris but is in fact living in pleasant obscurity somewhere in Europe; while Elvis Presley is not only alive but is regularly witnessed in unlikely locations throughout the Western world — a true case of the King being dead, but no one allowing him to die.

Yet all of this is not to suggest that President Kennedy or anyone else of his kind was part of an occult/political system which ensured a ritual murder according to a primordial pattern. What I am suggesting is that there exists within our consciousness a matrix akin to that found within solutions of copper sulfate, which causes crystals to take shape in the same general form every time. These matrices, or inner structures, are as old as time — and in fact time is the agent which is instrumental to their formation. The myth and lesson of the Sacred King is fundamental to Western consciousness in one way or another and finds expressions in the most unexpected but clearly recognizable ways. John F. Kennedy had to be assassinated, for the death of a sex god, like that of a sex goddess, should always be extraordinary. It is the least we demand of them. Slow decay is not for them, nor increasing decrepitude, so that generations come along to wonder what we ever saw in them. It is the sudden exit at the height of their erotic power which makes us remember and even revere. Fans of Marilyn Monroe, with whom he was connected, will understand that.

To understand this fully, we must now begin to look at something of the history behind it all, and learn that there are ancient sources of energy behind each and every individual. These energy sources can be drawn upon as needed — and they sometimes radiate into our lives whether we are aware of them or not ...

In ancient days the King was divine. The King was

God — or God's representative on Earth. And the King was also of the people. In prehistoric Britain, there were as many kings as there were tribes. They reigned in their multitudes over a multitude of kingdoms. During the time of their reign, each King was protected and cosseted by his people. Nothing was too much trouble. So if the King wished for something within the possibilities of their simple world, it was granted him. In many and strange ways they worshipped their own particular King; and then, at the specified end of his reign, they slew him, and spilled his blood upon the ground in order to revitalize it, tore his body apart (perhaps even ingested some of it), and then invested his eager successor with whatever trappings of regency they possessed.

> Romulus, the legendary founder of Rome, was said to have been cut to pieces by the patricians, who carried the pieces away under their robes and buried them in the earth. A similar custom was practised in early Scandinavia; King Halfdan the black was drowned in the spring when the ice was breaking; his body was divided into three pieces, one piece being buried in each of the three provinces of his kingdom.[1]

Once again the Osirian matrix-machine has been set on replay.

Even the passionate urge to remove the internal organs from the Sacrificed King is a direct echo of the Egyptians' removal and storage of internal organs in the mummification process. If an individual, community, or province could share in the substance of the King, they would necessarily come to express his innate fertility also. In the earliest of European cultures this

inner aspect of kingship — which may or may not have
derived from an Osirian original — was to be perpetuated for immense periods of time.

There are hints also, that, in some earlier cultures,
the actual powers of kingship were portioned between
two figures, whom we might term the Bright and Dark
Twins — which echoes certain concepts connected with
the magic of Sirius. The Bright Twin had all the regal
powers, all the outward authority that we traditionally
associate with the crown; but he was balanced and
supported at all times by the Dark Twin, the shaman
figure who expresses the inward side of the tribal mind,
and who more than anyone else maintains and clarifies
the links with the ancestors and guiding spirits. In a
sense, they were akin to the left and right sides of the
brain, together helping the tribal consciousness function as a single unit.

The sacrifice was made at the end of a specific period
of time, in accordance with certain stellar configura-
tions. It was almost unheard of for the victim to refuse
to be sacrificed. In any case, death in those days was no
more than a door through which the soul entered the
innermost Mysteries of the Earth; and so the victim was
soon able to peep back out at his tribe again from the
other side.

It was the Dark Twin who did the slaying, he who
guided the Bright King's spirit through its passing. In
later years, in societies that were very different, and
under kingships which were more truly national in
scope, the Dark Twin became the Divine Substitute. In
order to preserve the (successful) King's term, the Dark
Twin offered his life in exchange. This, we might
presume, was the real origin of a concept and practice
that later degenerated into the medieval use of "whip-
ping boys" who received those punishments more

properly due to young princes to whom they were bound from birth.

In later eras (and we are talking in terms of millennia now), it was felt that the King had to die not only as a means of ensuring continued fertility, but as a means of cleansing the people of evil.

There was a dim reflection of this in the last century, an old folk-memory which asserted that the way to avoid disease in a herd of cattle was to single out one cow and slaughter it in a ritually appropriate manner. Whatever portions of bad luck were due to the herd or its owner would thus be confined to just one clearly identified beast, so the rest would be left alone. We find continuing echoes of this in our own lives, too, when some poor wretch in our neighborhood falls prey to some disaster in the form of illness or accident. Underneath the concern, underneath the compassion, hidden away behind a natural desire to help the person or their family in any way we can, there is also a very deep and ancient hope that malignancy, like some ravening beast, has chosen its prey — your own family can survive for another year at least.

In purely psychological terms, the Divine King made extraordinary sense. No one could, or would, begrudge the wealth and trappings of regal power knowing that whatever rancors might develop, whatever hates or jealousies or grievances might arise, all would be redressed at the moment of sacrifice when the King, as a man, would get his "comeuppance." We can tolerate a lot from our leaders if we can be assured of that. This is, of course, the question of Nature being balanced, of things being put to rights, and justice being done. It is Maat in action.

Problems only arose when a King proved particularly good and well-loved, and no truly adequate successors could be found at the end of the reign, which usually lasted seven years. In an ideally functioning world, that successor would himself be "of the blood" — perhaps not necessarily as a direct offspring, but certainly possessing that peculiar spark which gave the Divine King his singular radiance. It was the furtherance of this spark, this genetic heritage, which caused the pharaohs to sleep with their sisters. This idea also caused the kingship in many Celtic tribes to be passed on from the King to the son of the King's sister — at least, they argued, you would always be certain who the mother was, but perhaps not the father. It should be remembered also, that King Arthur's only son was the result of a union with his stepsister. So when there was no obvious candidate for the successful King's successor, the Dark Twin himself became the Divine Substitute, and the reign could be extended a further seven years.

> The sacrifice took place in one of the Sacrificial months of the Old Religion, February, May, August or November ... As he was led to his death the streets and roads were often filled with crowds, weeping, mourning, and lamenting; cloths dipped in his blood and chips of the bloodstained scaffold were carried away as sacred relics credited with healing powers. The body was dismembered and the parts distributed to different places in the country in exactly the same way as the body of the Divine King was distributed.[2]

This is all part of the pattern. A pattern which has existed for so long that it has become intrinsic to our Western inner structures in one form or another, It is a pattern which states "that a God must die for man to live, good must deliver evil, the best of blood be shed to

redeem the worst, and the Sacrificial cycle be perpetuated to the end of time."³

As was shown in the beginning of this book, the
earliest pharaohs, who were manifestations of Horus in
life, and Osiris in death, were thought to be ritually
murdered by the Priest of Anubis at the end of an
extraordinarily long period which few probably
reached. No doubt this period of 28 years was the final
enactment beyond which no pharaoh was allowed to
rule. In the interim, he had the Apis Bull.

Osiris was the "Bull of Amenti" (the Underworld)
and, in his connection with Apis, the bull Fertility God,
he became Serapis, and was intimately associated with
the cycle of creation, death, and resurrection. Serapis
was both a Heaven-God and God of the Underworld.
The actual bull was found in a manner reminiscent of
the way the Dalai Lama is discovered: Priests were
appointed to search the land for a bull bearing all the
necessary distinguishing marks. The bull itself was
always black; there would be a triangular (or square)
patch on its forehead, double hairs on its tail, and the
sign of an eagle on its back, somewhere. All Egypt
rejoiced when a new Apis was found. When this
happened, the old bull was ritually slaughtered, its
flesh eaten, and its remains mummified in the royal
manner. It was finally buried with great ceremony at
Saqqara, in the building known as the Serapeum. This
last was an underground structure begun in the 18th
Dynasty, where the lives of the bulls were carefully
recorded. In later Dynasties, the Apis bull was kept in a
courtyard near the south gateway of the sanctuary of
Ptah at Memphis. Here he was enthroned and honored.
His advice, presumably channelled by his priests, was
eagerly sought, because he was thought to possess
oracular powers. In artistic representations he was

shown as a bull-headed man standing with his legs apart, wearing the Moon-disk within the crescent Moon and surmounted by two large plumes. He wore a breastplate on which were two cobras, and he carried the royal insignia of Osiris.

He was Osiris incarnate — the Horned God. We know him well by now.

One of the major figures from Egyptian legends, as opposed to pure myths, was Kha'm-uast. He was the eldest son of Rameses II and high priest of Ptah in Memphis, where he was presumably the major channel for the Apis-spirit. This type of shamanistic role may seem inconsistent with the popular notions of Egyptian magic, but in fact it has been analyzed at some length already in Billie John's brilliant exegesis of Kha'm-uast as a true Initiate.[4] In many ways, he was the Egyptian Merlin, a master magician of awesome powers. Had it not been for the supreme longevity of his father, he would certainly have become pharaoh — and a wondrously "winged pharaoh" at that. As it was, apart from his role as overseer of all the religio-magical ceremonies of the Upper and Lower Kingdoms, with a status similar to that held by the Archbishop of Canterbury in England, he had the Serapeum as something akin to his own temple, where the Apis bulls and the spirit(s) behind them surrounded him daily. In death, he was actually entombed with them. Kha'm-uast, High Priest of a Horned God, was to emerge from his tomb almost three thousand years later to start teaching the art of High Magic to a whole new breed of aspirants in the 20th century. He knew how to die all right, and exactly where to die.[5]

With this reference to Archbishops, we can return with some necessity to the theme of *The Divine King in England,* which is the title of Margaret Murray's seminal and brilliant book. The Archbishops of Canterbury, she asserted, were meant to be rather like those Dark Twins already mentioned. They were meant to hold and mediate the spiritual energies, and deal with the inner life of the nation, while at the same time they were to act, as the occasion and monarch demanded, as the Substitute.

The details of these historical relationships have been recounted extensively by Dr. Murray's admirers, so we need do no more than outline them here. It is a magical fact that if the reader really *needs* to learn about these Divine Kings and their Substitutes at some length, then the information itself will appear "as if by magic" from other perfectly natural but no less surprising sources. For our present purposes, we need only say that Dr. Murray's analyses are given in convincing detail.

There was Thomas Becket, Divine Substitute for Henry II, Dunstan likewise for Edwy, Lanfranc for William the Conqueror, Anselm for Rufus, and perhaps Henry VIII's three beheaded Chancellors for him. To this, we could add Joan of Arc and Gilles de Rais, who perhaps acted in a similar capacity for the French King. So not only Archbishops, but other souls close to the King in question and probably from certain "special" families — "victim" families in a sense — served in this way.

Murray cites a considerable amount of evidence for the validity of her thesis — evidence which is either derided by the orthodox historians as "vapid balderdash," or else unequivocally accepted by those of a more occult or unorthodox inclination. In the matter of the Sacred Kings, however, like in all occult topics, there is overwhelming evidence for those who believe but never remotely enough for those who wish to remain skeptical. Yet Dr. Murray was, I would insist, substantially correct. Her mistake — if it can be called that — was in writing purely from the point of view of the historian and anthropologist and taking no cognizance of the possibility that such patterns repeat themselves on a mythic level throughout history, without needing the back-up of covert pagan societies interweaving their rites throughout the orthodox structures of the time. The story of Kennedy's assassination is a case in point. *The Divine King in England* perhaps fails in the author's attempt to impose her thesis beyond the Tudor dynasty, even suggesting that Oliver Cromwell, of all people, made certain agreements with the Old Religion that she felt was still ruling from behind the scenes.

Still, she may have been right.

She did point out, almost in passing, that certain historical personages in certain parts of Britain were more closely associated with the Divine King concepts than in others. Perhaps because the priests in those areas were more literate, and able to record it all. She referred, for example to the Os kings of Northumbria: Osbald, Osbert, Osfrith, Osred, Osric, Ostrith, Oswald, Oswin, and Oswulf. Northumbria's spiritual power was and is derived from the isle of Lindisfarne, a tiny and mystical landmass which can be reached by foot twice a day when the tide recedes. According to the magician W. E. Butler, the power-source of Britain was to be found in Glastonbury; the love-aspect of the nation's psyche was held by Iona, an island off the west coast of Scotland identified with St. Columba; and Lindisfarne was the source of the wisdom-aspect. Not everyone accepts this, but at least it provides some people with certain angles to work on. The sources of these Kings' temporal power were often divided between Bamburgh — that serpent-rock place already mentioned — or

Yeavering, further inland. But they all acknowledged the peculiar sanctity of Lindisfarne.

Os is the Saxon rune ᚠ . (This rune had an earlier form ᚁ .) The names of these Northumbrian kings were thus to be regarded as titles: Osbald — Bold God; Osbert — Bright God; Oswulf — Divine Wolf, and so on. *Os* was thus a reference to the God, as far as they were concerned, a specific identification with Odin — he of the one eye and the Wild Hunt, who found his wisdom in the tree Yggdrasil whose branches conceal four harts. They held Odin within their names in the same way that pharaohs took on the syllables of Osiris. In this last factor we find a sonic coincidence that fits our scheme perfectly.

But these were obscure figures, admittedly little kings from a small realm. To get onto more national levels, and those with international and eternal relevance, we have to look at some of the larger figures in history.

But what must be realized first is that in medieval times Britain was a multi-ethnic society much as America is today. At varying times, the inhabitants comprised Angles, Saxons, Jutes, and the Brythonic and Goidelic Celts, who were to sort themselves out as the Scottish, Irish, Welsh, and Cornish peoples — all with their own dialects of Celtic. These were interlaced with people of Roman origin who were likely to have come from any part of the vast Roman Empire and who regarded themselves as the true aristocrats regardless of what hard times they may have fallen on after the legions left. Then there were regular and substantial influxes of refugees, traders, travellers from Brittany, Normandy, the Holy Land, and, generally speaking, all points east of Dover and south of the Isle of Wight and north of Lindisfarne. The very name England was said to derive from the God Ing, who has been equated with the fertility God, Freyr. His twin sister and sometimes consort, Freya, is often depicted riding on a broomstick, or a cat. The English became a homogeneous people only slowly, and only after the momentous Battle of Hastings in 1066.

After this Norman Conquest, it was never invaded again until World War II when something like a million G.I.'s came to delight our womenfolk with their bubblegum, bucks, and — as many satisfied females were happy to imply — their apparently insatiable sexual appetites. The Battle of Hastings put the lid on a melting-pot, just as Ankh-f-n-Khonsu once put the seal upon an Aeon. Hastings was the enactment between nations of the kind that should really have only occurred between the Twins. When one man tries to sustain his power and dynasty at an unnaturally high and unyielding peak, and when he creates laws, armies, and societies which all have the perpetuation of this power as their sole aim, then war is inevitable result. War is a perversion of the Horned God's rule, even if it sometimes necessary and tinged with the justice of Maat. War spills the blood of the common man upon the ground to ensure the continuation of the King and the King's seed, and the King's status. But the Divine King spills his own blood upon the ground for the furtherance of his people and their seed — and, in the purely agricultural sense, of their seeds.

Hastings was a conflict that was never inevitable, or even necessary, but it imposed grave changes upon the world. It was a conflict that was, perhaps, not so much about land and wealth and lust — although all of these played prominent parts — but about a religion that was quite new, and another that was indeed very old. Therein lay the real battles,

Americans take heed. One way or another it will happen there too, although on inner rather than outer levels.

Edward the Confessor is a good enough figure to start with: lean and lugubrious, tart, and often melancholy, with enough culture, elegance, sanctity and religion to make everyone suspect that he was not the paragon of Anglo-Saxon manhood. In no way did he fulfill any of the criteria for being the Horned God's representative on Earth — for, despite his marriage, he was a complete failure between the sheets. The marriage was almost certainly a chaste one, and, toward the end of his life, he spoke of his young wife in such glowing terms that none of his contemporaries could doubt that he had never touched her.

The cult of the Sacred King had probably ceased in England by this time. He was never "sacred" in the Pagan sense of the term. It may have ceased a generation before him, even, by the time of King Cnut, known more popularly as Canute. This was the king who was supposed to have tried to command the waves as an act of madness. But the truth of it was that Cnut (a very decent king) was actually trying to show his courtiers that he was not divine, but a mere mortal, and that the tide would wet his feet like those of any man. The first schoolboy version shows Cnut as an idiot; the second adult revision portrays Cnut's people as idiots. Perhaps he was just trying to show that no matter what they had been used to with previous kings, and no matter what they expected, he, Cnut, a Danish King ruling England, was not a God. Not for him were the sacrificial death or the apparently cruel Gods of the Old Religion.

That is one possibility. Details are so scarce that, by use of those magical words "perhaps," "possibly," "may have been," and "it may well be," we can turn it into what we want.

But there was no mistaking Edward's vision on his deathbed, which was recorded carefully by his attendants. They did this partly because he had a reputation for visions and minor miracles, but also because they were desperate for some sort of clue as to who his successor should be, As he slipped in and out of his delirium during January of 1065, he had one dream/vision which had enough impact to rouse him into a few final moments of lucidity. In this, he saw two long-dead monks he had known years before in Normandy. They were warning him that, because of the wickedness of the earls and churchmen of England, the country was about to be cursed: Devils would ride through the land with fire and sword and war. God would only cease to punish England when a green tree, felled halfway up its trunk and the top part taken three furlongs away, would join itself together again by its own efforts, without the aid of man, and break into leaf and fruit again.

His attendants looked hard at each other and had much discussion later. Yet surely it was not entirely symbolic. Edward had spent many of his younger years in Normandy, and he had said just enough to his hosts to suggest that the throne might, just might, go to the Duke of Normandy. His final words of warning, I would suggest, had less to do with clairvoyance than with a clear knowledge of the sort of man the Duke of Normandy was, and of the sort of God — or in his eyes, Devil — that the man and all his forebears followed.

William the Bastard was the son of Robert the Devil — nicknames which did not offend the bearers in the slightest. It was recorded that, at the end of the 10th century or at the beginning of the 11th, the Devil, in the likeness of the Duke of Normandy, came to the Duke's wife in a wood, and as a result of this union, she bore a son who was known as Robert the Devil.

We have a sense of *deja vu* here. Surely this is another aspect of that semi-divine shape-changing which results in someone rather special. Uther did this with Ygraine; Nephthys did this with Osiris. The Duke's wife, we might imagine, was in the wood in the first place to do more than gather berries. She was there for the sacred mating, the hierosgamos. It was the Horned God's representative upon earth with whom she mated.

Robert the Devil in turn married a woman known as Herleve, or Arlette, the daughter of a tanner in the town of Falaise, but by the time of the ceremony they had already had a son, William the Bastard, a name which he bore as a simple description of his status.

William the Bastard himself was to marry a woman named Matilda. All her other qualities apart, Matilda is worth mentioning here if only because of her size. When her tomb was opened in 1967 she was found to be just over four feet tall. Was she one of the fays? She was; I know she was.

The Normans as a people were, like the English, partly of Viking stock, although England had been invaded mainly by Danish Vikings, while Normandy received the brunt of Viking invasions from Norway. The differences between the two nations were marked: England was as settled and stable a country as any in Europe could be, whereas the Normans at that time were swept up by the primitive cults of horsemanship and war which would, in the following century, take shape as that international brotherhood known as chivalry, under which the great romances were about to be created.

It is said, with some degree of truth, that every nation gets the sort of leader it deserves. England had The Confessor to act as an incarnation of its spirit. The Normans had The Bastard. Born in the year 1027 or 1028, William was a man who was very rigid, very cruel, very powerful — in all senses — and who cared nothing about what people thought. Probably illiterate, he had all the diplomatic niceties and the political refinements of Attila the Hun. Even if he did, on occasion, resort to Christian law to gain support for his schemes, he was in no sense of the word a Christian.

When Edward the Confessor died, he was actually staggered to hear that, far from the English proclaiming him as the new king and eagerly lining the shores awaiting his triumphant arrival, they had actually crowned someone else in his place! He did the only thing he understood well: he gathered his army and prepared for war ...

The crown of England had actually been claimed by Harold Godwinsson, who was everyone's favorite, the complete opposite of The Bastard. Harold was patient, kind, charismatic, learned — and as hard a fighting man as could be found anywhere in the world. He was the leader of the house-carls, a small and professional army of men who were so tough that even a saga from Norway, homeland of the Vikings, told how one English house-carl was worth two soldiers from anywhere else in the world. They fought on foot, with swords and two-handed axes. And, with their backing, Harold prepared for the invasion he knew would surely come — not just from William in the south but from Tostig in the north, who was Harold's halfbrother and yet another rival to the throne.

The rest of the story is clear enough. Harold, waiting for the Norman fleet along the length of the southern English coastline, received news that Tostig and a massive Viking army had landed in the northeast. After a heroic march, his tired and outnumbered army nevertheless massacred the enemy, devastating them so completely that centuries of Viking raiding ended at that moment, on the bloody fields at Stamford Bridge. Harold and his army had no sooner sat down to lick their wounds than they heard the bad tidings which proclaimed that The Bastard's army had landed on the beaches near Hastings, some 300 miles to the south. Already exhausted, they made that journey, on foot, within five days.

The Bastard won, of course. The world knows that now. But only just barely, and only because the English had little strength left after Stamford Bridge, let alone the long marches before and after, and because the Normans had luck. They had also re-discovered the stirrup, which enabled them to fight from horseback in a way that the house-carls could not match.

And then, Sacred King claiming his rightful crown or not, The Bastard and his armies proceeded to loot, burn, and murder with an intensity that no one, least of all the existing worshippers of the Old Gods, could have believed possible. That part of him, we might believe, was *never* a true expression of the Horned God.

As for Harold Godwinsson, how should we regard him? Elected King? A true Christian King? Or someone just quick to seize a chance? Whichever, there are mysteries about him and his origins which are not easily resolved, given the scanty documentation. But what is certain is that, with this terrible battle, this spilling of Norman blood upon English soil for the purpose of a holy war, a link was created between the egregors of the two nations — still today, natural enemies. This link has joined them in a manner akin to the way the Bright and Dark Twins of yore were connected.

We can attribute two nice touches to William, however, before we move on to study his son as an unquestionable example of a Divine King. When he first set foot on the English beach, he sprawled his length before his omen-conscious and aghast followers. Undaunted, he rose and cried, "By God's splendor, I have seized the soil of England in both my hands!" In fact, he did this deliberately, echoing Julius Caesar who had said the same when landing in Africa. Three hundred years after William, King Edward was to echo both of them when he landed in Normandy on his way to slaughter the French at Crecy. While in 1944, on the Normandy beachheads — the choice of which had at least been partly suggested to the Allied commanders by Winston Churchill, who thought it historically apt — the same deliberate sprawl and same words were to be exclaimed by General George Patton, who was a man wracked by more than a few mystical notions himself. William knew that he was the focus of destiny at that moment, on the beach near Hastings where Aleister Crowley would one day go to die. He knew that he could *make* his omens. Some people have the knack of being able to see the future in the short term; others have the ability to shape it.

The second touch was that William had the pieces of Harold's body (had it been ritually dismembered?) wrapped in a purple cloth and buried under a heap of stones on a cliff-top overlooking the Channel. A stone was put on this simple grave bearing the following epitaph:

By command of the Duke, you rest here a King, O

Harold That you may be guardian still of the shore
and sea.

That, as one commentator rather snootily put it, was
certainly not a *Christian* act. "One is left to guess that
bond the burial signified between William and his
nation, what old, pre-Christian magic he felt he had to
propitiate."[6]

It was the Gods of the nation he had to deal with first.
The people, he would attend to later. Pagan or not, he
was a terrible, terrible man.

The true symbols of the Divine King are all to be
found more clearly in William Rufus, and less specula-
tion is needed in his case because the documentation
has survived in enough detail to support the thesis. But
one final thing that must be considered about the time
of William the Conqueror is his creation of what became
known as the New Forest, at the end of the 11th
Century. The forest itself, with all its scattered villages
and isolated dwellings, already existed, of course.
William's "new" forest involved not so much the
planting of trees as the complete and savage extermina-
tion of the existing inhabitants and the implementation
of unbelievably harsh laws against trespassers. This
was all so that the New Forest could become an
exclusively royal hunting ground — the chief prey being
the stag. Stags have always, in Europe at least, been
royal animals. The people could certainly see within the
behavior of stags a fine model of human kingship, in
which the dominant stag is challenged yearly for the
leadership of the herd in combats which were more
ceremonial than actual. They roamed free within the
New Forest, and they were hunted by the King.

The Egyptians, who lived in a narrow land with
strict limits to its fertile boundaries, had the Serapeum

as the home of their Sacred Bull, which was a living representative of the pharaoh and thus their God. Moved by the same impulse, though in very different forms, the New Forest was a vast and natural version of the Serapeum where the royal deer — never creatures for captivity — could run free and yet be available for the sacred rites of the King.

Even today, the New Forest, crisscrossed as it inevitably is by roads and heavy traffic, still retains its "witchy" reputation. Indeed, its influence upon the West has not really been considered fully. Samuel Liddell Mathers, the genius behind the Hermetic Order of the Golden Dawn, was born and brought up in what were then small towns on the edge of the New Forest. A generation after him came Gerald Brousseau Gardner, whom many regard as being the major influence in bringing Witchcraft back into the world again, and who received his initiation into the Craft in the Mill House near Highcliffe, at the hands of Dorothy Clutterbuck.[7] These two men, "coming to magic" on the edge or in the depths of the New Forest, generated two streams of light that have illuminated us all. Any modern magician who has ever studied the Qabalah, or "risen on the planes," or made the Enochian Calls, or used the banishing ritual of the pentagram; any witch who has ever adored the Book of Shadows, called down the Moon, or drawn circles with the athame, owes a debt of some sort and at some level to these two men. There was Mathers, in whose Order the supreme ritual involved him assuming the God-form of Osiris and rising from the coffin to awaken the inner mind of the candidate for initiation. And there was Gardner, amazed to find that those rites of the Horned God, assumed forgotten for centuries, were in fact being practiced within some English glades. Beyond them, and binding them, were the vibrant forces of the New Forest, which covers an area considerably less than that of any moderately sized American city. Beyond that is the image of the appalling man who made it.

One day America will have its own Mathers, its own Crowley, its own Gardner and Dion Fortune. It will have its own Bastard too, and medieval patterns will work themselves out from the hearts of its own countryside, and worlds and futures will be formed because of this. It was also in the New Forest that William Rufus, known as William the Red to those less scholarly, met his clearly sacrificial death as an Incarnate God of the Old Religion. If his father had made many enemies among the people by his method of of re-imposing the Old Ways with a sword, then the wounds had been healed by the time Rufus was to die on their behalf while hunting a stag. They came to his funeral in their masses. The common folk adored him ...

William Rufus was born in 1056 and crowned King of England in 1087. He was an open mocker of Christian shrines and made a hobby of destroying their churches. He was a King who dealt with law-breakers and villains of any sort with the kind of ferocity that would have made Edward the Confessor faint. But he was one who at least, as the old dream goes, made the country safe for women to walk out alone at night. That was some King. He was the sort of King, in fact, who exemplified the notion that "severity, consistently applied, breeds less discontent in the kingdom than mercy randomly administered." Never one to forget a good deed done to him or able to forgive a wrong one, he knew that he was able to justify all things in the eyes of his people by the fact that he was going to die the Old Way — a death which he finally approached with all the courage of a samurai.

On the eve of Lammas, which today is August 1st, sacred to the Bright God of Summer, William stayed awake all night chatting to his chamberlains. On the fateful morning, he dressed carefully and spent the early hours arranging his affairs, eating and drinking well and heartily. As he was being dressed for the hunt, a smith brought him six new quarrels — the short and stubby arrows used in the crossbow. Smiling, he handed two of them to Sir Walter Tyrrel, saying: "It is right that the sharpest arrows be given to him who knows how to deal deadly strokes with them." And then later, to the same man, he said with real gravity of manner: "Walter, do thou justice according to those things that thou hast heard!" To which Tyrrel nodded and replied: "So I shall, my lord."

In the forest, that New Forest which had been all but cleared of any unncessary inhabitants, the King became a leader of the Hunt indeed: the Wild Hunt which sought himself, and no other. It was not until the sun was setting that a suitable stag was seen, and William's bowstring broke. He then cried to Tyrrel: "Draw, draw your bow for the Devil's sake and let fly your arrow, or it will be the worse for you." Tyrrel did, and the arrow pierced the King. On being hit, the King uttered not a word but broke off the shaft where it projected on his body and fell upon the wound, which hastened his death.

According to one account, the body was found by a charcoal burner, placed in a rough cart, covered with a poor, ragged cloak and taken to Winchester, which was then one of the sacred cities of England, and probably had a population in the low thousands at most. In this account, great emphasis was placed upon the image of the King's blood dripping onto the ground during the whole journey — and although this is not possible it emphasizes the belief that the blood of the Divine King must fall upon the ground to fertilize it.

Rufus was not mourned by the nobles or ecclesiastics of that church he had so mocked in his lifetime, but by the common people. The poor, the widows, and the beggars came out in great numbers to meet the funeral procession and follow the King to his grave. It was their dead King, who had been the incarnation of their God, and the true regent of the common man.

His death was known in Europe within hours. No one is sure how this happened, although a Roman Legion-type signalling system has been suggested. Perhaps it was because they all knew he *had* to die at the appointed hour. Perhaps, with the elements of shaman-ism certainly active at that time, other communities simply *knew,* just as Aboriginal tribespeople even today can know that one of their members has had an accident, even hundreds of miles away. I knew when my mother died, on the other side of the country — a common enough experience. As an Englishman, I would expect to know about the death of my King. Certainly there is the tale — a hint to the common folk and fays — that the Earl of Cornwall, while walking in the New Forest, met a large hairy goat carrying the body of the dead King on its back. When questioned, the goat replied that it was carrying the corpse to the Devil for judgment. Here, surely, we can see a distorted version of the Horned God's priest in his ritual robes carrying the corpse away for the ritual dismemberment and/or feast.

We have to remember, too, that most of these were written down by clerics who would naturally interpret pagan rites in their own terms. When William cried: "Draw your bow for the Devil's sake!" we may be sure he was using the name of his own God, who Dr. Murray thinks may well have been Loki. Now Loki was once one of the supreme Gods of the Norsemen, but came to share that fate common to all Gods of his sparkling but darkling nature when he was later seen as a creature of pure evil. There was pagan blood in Rufus, all right. Whatever crimes had been committed in England by his forebears were expiated by his sacrifical act. As we are learning, the old saying "blood will out" has significance in more ways than we could have imagined before. We can leave the sacrificial genealogies of England to other writers who have already gone over this ground in exhaustive detail. In the magical way of things, those readers who actually *need* such detail will find the books in question.

The whole concept of the Sacred Kingship based upon carefully preserved bloodlines has been given a notable boost recently by *Holy Blood, Holy Grail,* a best-selling and highly controversial book which has, in fact, done no more than state publicly what many occultists had been saying for most of their lives: that Jesus did not die upon the cross, that he married Mary Magdalen, that their children were part of a bloodline which was to be perpetuated through the centuries. This secret dynasty was protected and nurtured by the mysterious Prieur[de Sion, an organization with (we are led to believe) enormous influence in the highest places, and a talent down through the ages for manipulating history.

We need not look with too much awe upon the Prieur[. Really, when we study the dark and furious history of Europe we can only conclude that the history-manipulators of the Prieuré were largely inept. Whatever glamour it might seem to possess can be banished at once with three simple words:

Belsen, Dachau, Auschwitz.

It is a question, also, of whether we accept Jesus as *the* Son of God, or a Son of Light. This in itself points out a peculiar advantage enjoyed by Pagans that not many of them realize: By regarding Jesus as a Son of Light — one of many — they can actually work with and appreciate much of the Christian Mystery Tradition while at the same time they never need to surrender their own pantheons. Christians, on the other hand, must necessarily accept the exclusivity of their God, and are forever denied the use of Pagan altars. It was because the followers of the Old Religion saw in the image of Jesus another example of a Divine King and Sacrificed God that they were quite happy let the new religion put down roots. To polytheists, or pantheists, one more Son of Light would not make much difference to their world. And Jesus, as a Thorned God, was just one more in a long line of such beings, even if he did *ascend* via his Father in Heaven rather than *descend* to the Underworld/ Otherworld/ Place of Ancestors as true Horned Gods invariably had to do. If the actual sacrifice, entailing the spilling of blood on the ground, was crucial to the mystery, it was equally supported by the necessity of the "divine dismemberment" which followed.

Just as Osiris' body was cut into fourteen pieces, and each piece buried in a different part of his kingdom, so can we find a very similar process at work in England — particularly as regards the head, which was regarded as the most sacred thing of all. When King Oswald of Northumbria was defeated in battle, his head was removed and placed first in the churchyard at Lindisfarne, and later removed to Durham. His body meanwhile was taken to Bordeaux in France, and then later back home to Gloucester. Somehow, one of his arms found its way to Peterborough — that town where the

first recorded sighting of the Wild Hunt was made —
and it was described as being "whole of flesh." This is a
common theme for all dead and mystical heroes — their
bodies do not decay. Like Egyptian mummies, they
remain whole and uncorrupted.

In fact, some of the kings were actually embalmed,
although the process was by no means as sophistcated
as that practiced in Egypt. When Henry I died, all his
internal organs were removed, the head was removed to
extract the brain (the Egyptians did so via the nasal
passages, using drills and hooks), and the eyes were
also taken out. The head was then sewn on the neck, the
corpse wrapped in ox-hides and taken to Caen, and
from there back to England to be buried at Reading. A
similar fate was recorded for Richard I, King John,
Henry V, and probably many others, including
Catherine of Aragon, who, Margaret Murray specu-
lates, was one of the women who refused to become a
Substitute for the King. (It was left to Ann Boleyn to do
this, a firm product of the Old Religion, who willingly
redeemed Catherine's lack of faith.)

The parallels between the English and Egyptian
systems are not exact, however, and admittedly these
may be circumstantial anyway. For one thing, England
was never as united as the Old Land. In an ideal realm,
in Avalon, the body of the King would be broken into 13
pieces (in Egypt, 14) and scattered throughout the 13
parts of the kingdom. Yet we can contrive to see a
possibility of this pattern in the 13 monastic cathedrals
served by regular clergy or monks. These are:

Bristol	Norwich
Carlisle	Oxford
Chester	Peterborough
Durham	Rochester

Ely   Winchester
Gloucester   Worcester
                  Canterbury

We could gloss over this but for the fact that
Peterborough is again so prominent. This is the place
where the dismembered parts of Kings and their
notional Substitutes are to be found, and where the
Wild Hunt was seen. At the time of writing this, in a
purely synchronistic, or "magical" coincidence, news
has appeared that archaeologists working at an indus-
trial estate at Peterborough have unearthed weapons,
jewelry, and skeletons almost 3000 years old, which
show the site to have one of the largest sacrificial
centers in prehistoric Europe.

Were all of those other cathedrals located at places
which had major magical significance in an era long
before the Christians came? Doubtless this was so. That
was the Christian way.

The process of dismemberment, and the distribution
of the parts to areas or individuals as a means of
bringing luck and fertility, is not so far removed from
the modern soul. There is a woman in a nearby town
who has, she insists, one of Elvis Presley's toe-nails,
found on a visit to Graceland. She now preserves it like
it was the Holy Grail itself. People today seek auto-
graphs and other mementos with the same intensity
that their forebears sought locks of hair, or limbs, and
for the same reason: as a means of relating to something
special, something or someone greater than themselves. In so doing they manage to feel they too have
become elevated toward the "stars."

All of this may seem far removed from the daily
concerns of the 20th century, but, as C. G. Jung said:
"Everything old is a sign of something coming." We

must look beyond the mere events to find the universal patterns within them, and thus touch those royal and divine aspects within ourselves. There is nothing intrinsically sacred about the Englishness of the historical events just described, for the patterns occur among all peoples in all lands. But they were at least put down on paper and recorded. This enables us to roll the details into crystal spheres for our own convenience and thus use the essence of history as a vehicle for prophecy. It is not infallible (prophecy never is) and is often relevant to no one beyond the individual, but it is a means of unlocking energies that will ultimately go beyond the individual and across the years.

Even the details of divine dismemberment and the places of storage can provide us with magic, for we can all try to link our associate parts with portions of the landscape. We can do this at a local level, such as apparently happened in the ancient Goddess-center of Avebury in Wiltshire, whereby the streams, valleys, hills and numberless megalithic remains were all expressions of the Goddess in her cycles from Maiden, Mother, to Crone. Or we can play our game again, trying to do this at a national level by identifying where a country's brain center is, or heart-center, and so on. We already do this unconsciously when we describe a particular place as being the "arm-pit" of the state, or even the asshole of an area. A crude game, perhaps, but one which can yield surprising results. We can also — and should also — do this within our lives: "My heart is in _____ because I grew up there; my head is in _____ because that was where I learned most; my strength is in _____ because I learned toughness there; and so on. In this sense, we have to think in terms of qualities rather than physical bits and pieces: compassion is your left arm, discipline your right;

career is your torso; and so forth. There can be no hard and fast rules to this, for you have to become your own Wild Hunt, chase yourself, and pull yourself apart. Some people, already torn asunder by life, have to become their own Isis in search of their own parts and learn to pull themselves together again.

This is the real magic, the true sorcery. We are all daily practitioners of the Old Religion if we could only see it. The spirit of Divine Kings is within us all.

Notes

[1]Margaret Murray, *The Divine King in England.* (London: Faber, 1964), p. 28.

[2]Margaret Murray, *The God of the Witches,* p. 160.

3Gray, William, *Sangreal Sacrament.* (York Beach, ME: Samuel Weiser, 1983).

[4]In preparation.

[5]Alan Richardson, *Dancers to the Gods.* (Wellingborough, UK: Aquarian Press, 1984) details the inner contact that existed between Kha'm-uast and two magicians of the 20th century.

[6]David Haworth, *1066: The Year of the Conquest.*

[7]Doreen Valiente, one of the most lucid commentators on modern witchcraft, was able to show in her long essay in *The Witches Way* by Janet and Stewart Farrar, that Old Dorothy did indeed exist, despite the scepticism of those commentators on the subject who have prided themselves on their "balance" and their rationality.

[8]Perhaps one of the candidates for the American Presidency may have been less keen to change his name beforehand if he had been aware of such patterns. Hounded from the race by media which pilloried his sexual appetite as well as his identification with the Kennedy-image, Gary Hart must sometimes have wondered at the true natures of the forces he unleashed.

The Time of the Wakening

The Old Religion never really died, as so many thought. Christianity never really triumphed in any absolute sense. What happened was that the Horned Gods and Goddesses of each region "passed on" in the truly magical, rather than the purely euphemistic, sense. In mythological terms, they disappeared into the hills, just as the fays went into their mounds, and just as humanity today (if the worst thing happens) will take to the nuclear bunkers. Like Osiris, the Horned God took up his place within the Underworld. There he waits for the True Son to claim his helm and perform a sort of Ritual of the Opening of the Mouth, whereby the ancient energies would spring forth again, and the Old Gods speak.

The Horned God and his rites and representatives withdrew by necessity. Conditions on the land were changing rapidly. This perhaps was coupled with the increasing development of that left-brain consciousness unable to perceive the natural forces and the ancestors as having direct and living impact upon the

individual. Christianity, acting as something of the
Dark Twin, did no more than rip out the heart of an already dying sacrifice.

We could blame the introduction of the heavy plows,
which could accomplish in one day what it would nor-
mally take many men a whole week to achieve. We
could blame Pietro de Crescenzi for his *Opus ruralium
commodorum* (1304), which showed man how to control
the land by means other than magical propitation, and
at the same time we could direct some animosity toward
John Fitzherbert for developing these ideas in his book,
Husbandry. Later still, we could rail against the likes of
Messrs. Tull and Meikle, whose seed-planting machines and threshing machines completely revolution-
ized the harvest. Or we could blame the plagues which
devastated perhaps as much as half the popuation of
England alone, and altered the fabric of society forever;
or else we might cast a cold eye on those agricultural de-
velopments that took the small plots of land away from
the subsistence farmers and concentrated them in the
hands of a few powerful landowning individuals who
left the rest to machines. But most of all, in England at
least, we can blame the sheep. The demand for English
wool was so great, and so much money was to be made
from it, that vast areas of hitherto inhabited and culti-
vated land were turned over to the grazing of sheep.
This meant that the bulk of the population was driven
off the land and into the cities, causing Thomas More to
exclaim that: "The sheep have eaten up the men!" Natural cycles were forgotten; communities that had once
achieved a precious (and often precarious) self-
sufficiency through a kind of symbiosis with the land
and its seasons, were destroyed. Forests were leveled to
make yet more land for grazing. In time, the international demand for wool was to have as much impact

upon once-Merrie England as the discovery of oil was to
have upon the Arab nations. The Christians, who used
the Lamb as their totem animal, and who now saw the
Old Religion retreating everywhere, must have been
well pleased. They did their very best with the noose
and the burning faggots to help the process along.

It is at this period that we can catch glimpses of the
Horned God and his Goddess in full flight. Herne/
Gwyn, call him what you will, was reviled as the Foul
Fiend, the Enemy of Salvation, and a true Lord of Darkness. His influence was seen as malignant and deadly;
corruption and putrefaction were thought to mark his
every step. And no one could see that this was a symp-
tom of the ways in which Man's relationship with Nature had become corrupted — it was in this relationship
that the real putrefaction lay. A few places still did per-
servere with the old worship. The clerical authorities
made clear these were orgiastic ceremonies in which
the Devil and his Whore were adored, and at which un-
speakable sacrifices were made.

Three processes were at work here. The first is that
attitude already mentioned in which a society and its
priests had lost touch with the sensuous yet innocent
and joyous aspects of the old Fertility Cult, so that the
image of a free and running stag, for example, became
corrupted into the static and all-consuming goat which
best examplified the Christian interpretation. Second,
we can see the ultimate development of that technique
of religious conversion in which the gods of the former
religion become the devils of the new. And third, it is
true to say that some of the covens *were* actually involved in calling on forces of real darkness. Divorced
from the old cycles of Nature, living in a distraught
world where the tribes and (later) agricultural communities no longer existed, they sought wealth and power,

pleasure through whatever magical means beckoned them, using whatever techniques were deemed most potent.

This "corruption of images" can be seen in different ways. If the Royal Family of medieval England was no longer seen as Divine, and no longer acted out the great rituals, then members of the lesser nobility often took a Witch King mantle upon themselves. Presumably this was done through a kind of despairing Apostolic Succession down through the ranks. Thus Francis Stewart, Fifth Earl of Bothwell, the nephew of Mary Queen of Scots, was rumored to have been the very incarnation of the witches' Dark Lord. Bothwell was indeed a very dark man; if he was a true King of the Witches, it was a mantle he did not deserve.

The idea of living sacrifices offered to the Horned God is also a corruption of a far older and purer truth linked with that deity. This is not at all to be confused with the sort of willing sacrifice described in the previous chapter. The truth is simply that the Horned God will give things, but he will also take something away. This is that cosmic Law of Exchange which says, in simple terms: If you want something, you have to pay for it somehow. Matter can neither be created nor destroyed — it can only be swapped around a bit. Not only had humanity lost the living essence of their oldest God in the later centuries, it lost this knowledge concerning the exchange of spiritual energies. If we want things from the Horned God — knowledge, love, power — then we must be careful to consider what we might offer him *from within ourselves* in return. It is the subtlety of this exchange which holds many of the secrets of his awakening today.

This intuitive knowledge had all but disappeared by the time of the 18th and 19th centuries, although a few

individuals in remote parts of the countryside still possessed the sort of natural magical powers which singled
them out as witches. In visual terms, the only hints in
the world that there had ever been anything other than
a Thorned God were to be found in the "foliate heads."
These are church-carvings in which a human face is
seen peeping through foliage, or a face actually formed
from foliage, or one with foliage sprouting from the
mouth in a wonderfully Osirian manner. They could be
found carved on roof bosses, corbels, capitals, fonts,
tympana, tombs, and on wooden screens, bench-ends,
and misericords, and so on. All are likely to be seen in
any church with pre-1500 features. It is as though the
stone-carvers were determined to remember this figure
from the Old Worship even if no one else was.[1]

These faces were all that remained, at least in England, of that divine figure who had once brought fertility to the land. These, and all those folk-customs which
even the English themselves thought quaint, were like
the last reverberatioss of a once-powerful cry — the cry
of the rutting stag which goes *Her-Her-Hernaa, Her-
naaa*...[2] There was Morris Dancing and maypole dancing, ceremonies which involved circling churches or
tapping on trees to awaken them, little springtime rites
(often now with the full blessing of a secure and igno-
rant Church). Many of these customs related to springs
and wells and orchards, and the frequent appearance of
some local who was called "Jack in the Green" or the
"Green Man," and who appeared in a variety of
strangely Osirian forms; for example, in a wicker pyramid, or all covered in vegetation, or smeared in black as
Osiris was black when he was found in the silt of the
Nile. All these things were like those memories which
stick maddeningly on the tip of the tongue, impossible

to place, but with intense and evocative flavors nevertheless.

An 'Osiris bed' as found in Tutankhamen's tomb

It is with the title "Green Man" that we find ourselves most surely full circle, back to those impossibly
distant days in the First Time, as they called it, when
Osiris was the Green Man who taught his people how to
raise crops, cultivate vines, and make peace — that best
of all. Here was the true son of the Earth God who contained within himself the patterns of birth, growth,
death, and renewal on all levels, and in all ways. Here
was the figure who held the secret and source of fertility, both within the land and within the people who
worked that land. Sometimes, in small villages along
the Nile, they would honor him by fastening heads on

poles — heads made from corn and adorned with hair, feathers, and horns — in a reverential act that was no different from the folk-customs involving corn-dollies in old England, several thousand years later.

Whether we focus upon Herne or upon Osiris, in both cases their relationships are concerned with involving humanity in a direct and living relationship with the Earth, in particular with the specific geographies in which individuals conduct their lives, whether these are in the depths of the city or the heart of the forest. They can both teach us about the "spirit of place," and show us how we can learn from this to find the "place of spirit," and so take our positions in the dance of nature from which we have become sadly separated. They teach us the Law: as without, so within — there is no difference.

The fate of the earth itself hangs on how we learn to deal with the energies they focus.

We are at that moment in time now when Horus is visiting the inert and listless figure of his father who is lost within the Underworld and guarded (and also constrained) by monstrous serpents. His father, remember, has that "wound in the thigh" which has somehow been responsible for the wasteland in which he now lives. Horus is there to claim his crown as the Earth-God's true heir, but first he must perform that crucial ceremony known as "The Opening of the Mouth," using a small adze to help him. Once the mouth is opened, the life of the world will spring forth, as with the foliate heads, and a new cycle will begin. Osiris transcends his helplessness — he lives, and the Earth lives with him.

As above, so below — Horus and Osiris in balance.

Part of the ceremony involves Horus telling Osiris exactly what ails him. Osiris cannot be cured until that is done. It presupposes that the son is mature enough, and knowledgeable enough, to be able to speak with certainty about the world's ills.

Today, as we look upon our polluted oceans, breathe our polluted atmosphere, and watch the destruction of those natural resources vital to the ecosystem, we find the Horus-hawk alive within us, and completely horrified.

It is a start. It is *the* start.

But a cure for this land of waste and pollution cannot be effected unless Osiris wants to be healed. That is, unless we can find that spark within ourselves which tells us that "The Land and its People are One," and that the world's ills are a direct result of ills within ourselves, then no change will occur as a result. The story of Osiris is really one of supreme self-reliance, and of will and intent. Osiris, lost within the Underworld, has to realize that he can transform those monsters which threaten him and render him inert and turn them into his purest allies. Wer and Mehen, "The Most Ancient One" and the "Encircler" respectively, can be changed from being his serpentine captors into dragons on which he can soar.

The adze, or small plow, which Horus uses to set these outpourings of the New Age in motion,was seen as a symbol of the constellation of Ursa Major, the Great Bear. In the light of the peculiar historical relationship that exists between the peoples of the Eagle and the Bear, American magicians can afford to interpret this on whatever political levels they deem appropriate, given the most recent events.

To the British mind, however, the Great Bear is King Arthur pure and simple, and much occult work has been done in recent decades with the express intent of Awakening the King, and bringing in the Age under his aegis in some way. What magicians have aimed for as individuals or groups is a Second Coming, no more, and no less. Perhaps not in the focus of a single individual — which would be disastrous at a time when all invividuals have to learn to shoulder their own burdens — but via the incarnation of numerous highly-developed souls all attuned to a similar frequency, so to speak, and making their impacts in the realm of science in particular. But science with a heart this time.

The Serpent King from Abydos

In Arthurian/Celtic terms, the imagery and inner-plane energies known as Lancelot/Gawaine have cut those furrows into the soil of our consciousness. In these furrows, seed-ideas have been planted. While in the Egyptian system, it is Horus who will rule the new Aeon and restore Maat to the world. This is a case of the Hawk, which brings order back into the world, covered with and soaring by the feathers of Maat, and restoring humanity to a new balance with its environment.

The result, however, is not a foregone conclusion. Before that can happen, there will be yet more turbulence and bloodshed, more confusion and self-seeking. This is because humanity is now experiencing a surge of sexual energy and awareness comparable to what we as individuals know at puberty. This surge will make possible the crossing of the interval between hunanity's childhood and the onset of adulthood. But, as Maat would say, the whole thing hangs on a feather. It all depends on whether we can awaken the Horned God within us, so that the Hawk can soar and one day take us to the stars.

These stars, in fact, represent one of the few things that most magicians can agree upon. They argue that our true home is to be found among the stars, and that we do not really belong on this planet at all. Hence the profound feeling that many of us have that we are "outsiders." The true "Fall," they contend, was caused by "interbreeding between anthropoid humans and a far superior race from another solar system many millennia ago."

It is a glorious notion, but an uncomfortable one, given the lunatic fringe that such an approach immediately conjures up. However, it is made a bit more acceptable by the suggestion that these "star people" came to Earth *not* via spacecraft but as "viral infections," space-hardy germs. These could have been carried on meteors, perhaps. Each germ might then have characteristics that worked themselves into the genetic structures of the apelike creatures they infected.

I first heard this idea — or its cousin — over twenty years ago while sitting wide-eyed, young, and nervous in the cramped study of a formidable English magician who told me of this while cranking up the pressure on his antiquated paraffin heater. Years later, many years later, the highly regarded and utterly respectable astronomers Fred Hoyle and Chandra Wickramasinghe caused a minor controversy and swayed some pundits when they suggested much the same sort of thing as the most likely origin of human life and consciousness, as well as many epidemic diseases.

Other magicians, however, stick to the more usual notion in which Earth was visited and colonized by several intelligent races from distant star-systems, some of which had distinctly animal-like features — which accounts for the true origins of the Egyptian Gods. A gutsy modern magician, Murry Hope, acting as the medium for her Paschat, or "Lion People" communicators on the inner planes, says that the links are to be found between Earth and the systems of Andromeda, Auriga, Orion, and Sirius — especially Sirius.

However we look at it, and however it happened, it is asserted that the true Sangreal, or Blood Royal, sprang from some sort of contact with these beings. "This created a genetic strain which carried on the very best of human capabilities allied with good spiritual influences. This strain, it was felt, has considerably influenced our state of civilization for the better, inculcating an unusual element of self-sacrifice among its holders for the sake of spiritual immortality." And then further: "It was once regarded as exclusive to certain noble families, but long ago was known to have become extremely widespread, albeit in varying degrees in different individuals."[3]

Can we believe this? We can if we want. We can all find these stellar genes within us if we need to.

In the simplest terms, the Star-Seed/Sangreal/Blood Royal is energized at that moment when individuals, lost within the morass and terrorized by demons of their own making, decide that enough is enough, that they *must* rise, that there has to be something beyond or above to which they can relate. That is true initiation, and the beginning of all magic. The Star People can take care of themselves. For the moment, just getting out of the hole is the best that we can begin to do. Once we make this decision from the heart, then all systems and interpretations become unified: The Blood Royal begins to pulse within the veins, the antlers or horns begin to grow, the eyes of Osiris flicker open — and the dawn of a New Aeon begins perpetually anew.

Notes

[1]Janet and Colin Bard, *Earth-rites: Fertility practices in pre-industrial Britain.* (London: Collins, 1983).
[2]Observed by Doreen Valiente.
[3]William Gray, *op. cit.*

Endings and Beginnings

When I first met the Horned God, I was 24 years old, far younger than my years, newly married and already feeling doomed — and a prime example of what was once called a "callow youth." My one mark of distinction, as I thought of it myself, was an obsession with magic that had endured for most of my conscious life. But even here, although I had much knowledge, there was little wisdom; ample imagination but no real insight or understanding. I did not even know the Horned God existed, much less what he stood for.

My first wife and I were a couple doomed from the start: a Chinese pragmatist and a Celtic dreamer do not make the best of bedfellows, even if we did at times love each other with the sort of determination that is really the heavy lid that keeps down despair. I very much knew Atum in those days — we both did. Two dark mounds that occasionally signalled to each other across an emptiness. No faults, no wrongdoings, no recriminations — just different worlds.

In times like that, you tend to find the Horned God.

161

This is not so much through any process of occult
research, or magical evocation. It is more akin to the
way the Nile recedes, so that you feel as if all the vitality
of the dream world has drained away, and there is only
thick mud all around, and a cold, thin air where once
there had been the currents and shoals within the flow
of life itself. He is there, if you know how to look, if you
know how to brush off the mud and dirt.

It was in Earls Court arena in the heart of London,
where I first saw him: a vast cavern of a building where
they have dog and horse shows, boat and home
exhibitions, and where the Royal Family come once a
year to be dutifully bored to their back teeth by those
interminable military extravaganzas which the Old
Boys put on for their entertainment.

The Rolling Stones were in concert for that particular
occasion, however, and we had tickets, procured with
some difficulty. Not because we particularly liked the
Stones' music — I had always been a Cat Stevens, Bob
Dylan, Paul Simon man myself — but because we were
drawn to the myth. Everyone of my generation had to
see the Stones at some time. They were seminal. They
were definitive. They were 7 pounds a ticket.

Now the Stones were late in appearing, as they
always were. The thousands in the audience were
restless but good-humored. The mysteries of ancient
Gods were the *last* things upon my mind just then.

That was when the fanfare began. A sound of
trumpets echoed and echoed around the hall. I had
never heard the piece before and assumed it to be
something classical. Then, suddenly, it was all forgotten. Time and place gave way to one of the purest
visions of my life. Beneath the huge arch of the ceiling,
amid the indefinable but tangible atmosphere of
sexuality that was loose within the audience, within the

stink of smoke, and dope, and alcohol strong enough to support the roof, the Horned God came riding into my vision. Clear and potent and intensely alive, he came riding a dark horse from out of the depths of some primeval forest, into the bright sunlight at its edge. He looked at me across the worlds, across the years, and I was lost to him from then on.

Herne? I thought, or seemed to hear. Although I had little myth then, and less learning, the name was accurate enough, as we have seen. As the music of the fanfare rose and fell and faded away, a door leading to something wonderful opened within my psyche. The Crown of Thorns and all the associated Christian Mysteries ceased to bother me so much. Gradually, surely, it was the God with Horns who began to claim me.

For the rest of the evening in the outer world, Mick Jagger's prancing on stage around a huge, pink, inflating penis seemed rather silly and completely irrelevant. Moons had arisen within me and nothing was likely to be the same again. Part of me died, but part of me gave birth to something at the same time.

The music, as I later learned, was Aaron Copland's "Fanfare for the Common Man" — an entirely appropriate title, as I now realize. And in the light of the Fertility Cult which once rippled outward from the Horned God's image, Jagger's performance on stage was an unconscious piece of mediumship that aptly celebrated a lesser-known God.

He was alive that night within me. It was the best 7 pounds I ever spent.

He was to crop up again later, over the months and years, but most of the time he was forgotten completely in the need to live a normal life, try hard at marriage, and earn a living as any mortal has to. His most vital appearance actually came a few months after the first, bursting into my inner gaze in the lush gardens of the Manor Hotel in Castle Combe in Wiltshire — a village which had once been voted the prettiest in England, and suffered ever since. *Dr. Doolittle* had been filmed there, as I later learned. Which, considering the Horned God's role as Lord of Animals, was surely an example of the wry humor that only he can manifest. Really, it was a simple enough encounter: a tall friend of mine stepped under some antlers that were fastened onto a shed wall: but then he seemed to disappear and, for a brief and unforgettable moment, a priest from the oldest light stood before me, filled with the God.

But it was not until 1981, after my wife and I had bowed to the inevitable and separated — mercifully without children to complicate the matter — which the Horned God began to impinge upon my psyche on a regular basis. In fact, the pressure intensified toward the end of that year until I found myself staying awake night after night, filled with a compulsion to draw and re-draw his image in immense size but with tiny detail. I drew these with simple black and white lines without shading, without depth — which perhaps mirrored the state in which I then found myself in the lonely days before Michelle appeared. Such a compulsion to draw invariably marks the awakening of the right hemisphere of the brain, and is a signal that some greater mysteries are on the way. They were, and I attempted to write them up in an ultimately unsatisfactory book entitled *Gate of Moon*. For long nights in the heart of winter, within the heart of the Western Lands, I lived with the Horned God's image daily — with him and Fi n, which was the name to which his consort seemed to respond.

They never said anything in words. No axioms, no

precepts or philosophies. Yet they taught me things somehow, and I would wake from sleep with knowledge that was completely new to me, but which I felt I had known all my life.

Michelle came into my life then, and with her a radiance that was like a smile. She was thirteen years my junior but a thousand years older. I had last seen her in the 17th century when we had had a rugged and impoverished life as farmworkers, living near the village of Marshfield in Wiltshire. We buried as many children as we managed to raise. But before *that,* if we look at it in linear terms, we had shared a considerably brighter world beside the Nile, where I had been a minor scribe and she a young priestess. That night, in January of 1982, she turned up on my doorstep and asked me if I would like to take her for a drink. I would, and did, and our marriage and our children followed on at decent and entirely respectable intervals.

In those first years, we rented a tiny old cottage on the middle slopes of a steep valley, where a fold in the earth and a trick of the trees which encircled us gave the area a micro-climate all its own. It was always warm, snow never lasted more than a morning, and the wind through the trees further out made it sound like the ocean lapped to our door. Deer would come down the path; badgers and squirrels would dig out our crops; pheasants would strut upon our wall. Every now and again a great black dog would leap from nowhere into our garden and muzzle around as if it owned the place. While every night, as the Moon soared high above the hills, darkness and silence would encircle our home in a way that showed they were living entities too, deserving our acknowledgements. At two separate places within the large and rambling garden, I came across what I can only call the "Gates." Through these, on certain occasions, I was quite certain that I could have stepped right through into the faery realms — quite literally. Without a wife and child, I would have done so. In fact, I believe that these Gates and opportunities only open fully to those who *do* have such considerations and concerns. It is all part of the Law of Exchange.

It was during this period, when our first child was growing up and I was learning to use the elf-wands given me by Dusty Miller, that I seemed to have "plugged into" what I can only call the Pagan aspects of a Magical Current that was originally worked within the Stella Matutina, and which was (in many strange ways) linked to energies within the hill on whose slopes we lived. Synchronistic events of staggering scope and complexity, involving awesome levels of coincidence, unfolded with such frequency that I became almost blase. But at least I learned to take it all as a sign that the Horned God was alive and indeed a-hunting,

People accused me in those days, too, of being wonderfully psychic. So I was, and so I am, but I tell many more lies now than I ever used to. This is all part of the roguish, trickster, coyote aspects of Herne. It is really no great problem. The best magician I ever met was not averse to spinning the odd yarn or three.

Then Herne showed me that life on the land is never an idyll, that the least it demands is hard and unremitting graft, with no place for the arrogance of self-pity, or the luxury of despair. He showed me the dark and cold things too, without which the light can have no reality, nor the warmth any power to heal. But those are parts of another story, and not for anyone else. This too is part of the Law of Exchange, the Balancings of Maat.

It was not until the spring of 1989, long after we had left the cottage to live upon another part of the hill, that various strands of magic that had been bothering me for some time all seemed to coalesce at once, triggered by a "chance" encounter with a delightful lady witch of my acquaintance, who spent a few minutes chatting on a variety of topics while the lock of the nearby canal filled with the murky, black-green water. "Did you know," she asked, "that the well and spring near your village is known as the Spring of the Green Man?" I didn't, no I didn't. And it was like a blow to the head as a multitude of concepts and personal experiences which had apparently no relationship all came together at the same time. I went to the well in question, and the spring which flows from it, tidied up the debris, and sat back to build up the great and "green" images of Herne and Fiân, and sat on a rock and listened like a little boy while they spoke to me of their relatives and ancestors, and showed how they were all within me — within us all. So all that remains to do now is open a few doors, unlatch a few gates. The Horned God and his Lady do not ask a great deal from us in the way of actual techniques. They are not overly fond of dogma. On the whole, unless you catch them in the Osirian mode, they would rather not have the elaborate ceremonial that many magicians insist upon creating. In fact, they really only need two small things from us: a knowledge that they exist and a determination to make contact. Although perhaps we can add a third — the quality of respect. Not worship, not blind adoration, just simple and dignified *respect* is quite enough for any man, woman, or deity.

Knowledge and determination are the actual dynamics which will get us started via some exceedingly simple first steps. We need simply research the Horned God and his Lady in public libraries, draw their images — no matter how crudely — from whim and fancy.

While you do this look out for the stag/hart/deer/ram/ horned animal motifs in the outer world. Make a note of everything.

That is the start, nothing more. If you have the guts, the balls, and the "fire within," you will realize in later years that every step you make toward the Horned God, the Horned God is making toward you.

But you have to want this to happen with all your heart — with all of your hart.

Everyone's approach toward the Horned God must necessarily be different. The important thing is not what you do, or how cleverly you do it, but the fact that you are doing it at all. This is Osiris rousing himself, deciding that he must quit the night and come toward the day. This is Herne coming to the edge of the primeval forest, under a similar compulsion. It is Arthur — and any other sleeping hero — rousing himself because he knows that a time has come.

When it comes to raising the Horned God, the crucial factor depends on the efforts made by the seekers themselves — not via the specific techniques and formulae of an established cultus, but through their own ingenuity. It does not matter how crude and indeed silly the first attempts at making an inner contact are. It is the courage to make the attempt in the first place which the Horned God seeks. He will respond in kind. Do no more than slavishly copy the methods of established practitioners and all you will get is a kind of dull, Otherworld golem. Use your own creativity and you will touch upon the Horned God in the full flow of his power.

We could, strictly speaking, end the book here. Having read this far, each person now contains within him or herself all that is needed to set about making a genuine, transformative contact with our oldest deity.

Nevertheless, we would be accused, and with some degree of justification, of opting for the cop-out. What we can offer now, therefore, are some suggestions, a series of possibilities which initially require nothing more than a quiet place to sit and the ability to think and breathe at the same time. After a while, you won't even have to bother about the thinking part. They are deliberately given at random, in some instances. Deliberately not tied together in any neat and prepackaged manner. Rearrange, dissect, criticize, synthesize or expand them in any way you want. That which comes from within yourself is the only real magic there is ...

Return to Nothingness

We can attempt the return to "Nothingness, *Nun,* and Nowhere," in which we attempt to achieve something of this state as a (temporary) mode of being. In those techniques of Ceremonial Magic known as "banishing rituals," the real importance has little do with dispelling unwanted entities and more to do with creating a psychically clean atmosphere both within and without. In terms of the Qabalah, it is a means of simulating the state of *ain soph aur,* or Absolute Nothingness. In the by-now traditional magic of the Golden Dawn, for example, they would draw in the air the form of the pentagram in the four Quarters, invoke archangelic presences, and intone certain "words of power" and use other techniques. In later variants, based upon those three circles of Time, Space and Events, which link together like the rings of a gyroscope, this same state of "returning to zero" is accomplished with the aid of the intoned sonics "I.A.O." There are other methods — countless other methods. But we need not worry about them now, if ever. All we need for our own simple purposes is our names.

Begin with your own name and say it aloud three times, brooding upon your own sense of identity as you do so. Say it slowly, sonorously, and with intent. Then say it again, but without the last letter. And again, and again, removing a letter each time, and carrying with this the sense that your personality is being whittled away, your mundane consciousness with its perpetual internal monologue being diminished to the single essential spark. If you have learned anything about magic from other sources, and have created your own magical name, then you can use this technique with your everyday outer name first, and *then* do likewise with your chosen "inner name." We can see the whole process at work in that well-known medieval talisman aimed at identifying an illness with a magical word, and then reducing the illness by reducing the word:

> ABRACADABRA
> ABRACADABR
> ABRACADAB
> ABRACADA
> ABRACAD
> ABRACA
> ABRAC
> ABRA
> ABR
> AB
> A

There are many possibilities for this technique: diminishing problems, reducing worries, healing of various sorts — and getting back to the sort of singular, point-like consciousness which precedes most magical work.

It is an old and basic technique, but it works.

Becoming One with Atum

We might call this next technique "becoming One with Atum." Use it in conjunction with the former as you think fit. Look at the simple glyphs which represent Atum and the Aker. Build up an image of the desert within which the sphinx-like Aker guards the path toward the stepped pyramid which is the primeval Mound of Atum.

Between the paws of the Aker is a secret door through which only you can enter, but only after giving a particular sign — any sign which you have previously chosen as your particular key.

The passage behind the door leads ever downward beneath the earth. You float down it, and in due course you find yourself hovering loose and freely floating within the immensity of that pyramid whose tip, you now realize, had only just broached the surface of the upper world. Feel the nature of this pyramid. Sense the angle and shape of the distant walls and the way that the energies both converge toward and radiate from the top.

You must intone: *Atum, Atum, Atum,* as deeply and resonantly as you can. Imagine it echoing off the walls. Just feel, and sense: don't analyze or interpret. *You* are now, in a very real sense on magical levels, the master of this castle of primeval forms. The darkness around you is not darkness: you can make it want you want.

Now this, when used in conjunction with the first technique, can in itself prove an extraordinary experience. It is inevitably brought to a halt when concentration flickers and the internal monologue breaks through again. But nevertheless it can — if only for a few brief if timeless seconds — give you a sense of your own essence, and clear away much of the "debris" which prevents other beings from making their presence felt.

The steps of the pyramid itself can be regarded as the steps and stages of your outer life: childhood, adolescence, adulthood, plus all the aspects which add to these stages such as parents, friends, children, all colored by the major events such as having sex, marriage, giving birth, experiencing the death of loved ones, and so forth. Each of these steps or stages can be felt as expressing themselves in the realms of the instincts, intellect, emotions, and intuition. The pyramid, therefore, is a symbol of life as it is expressed in the material world. You, the spark, are in there somewhere, learning to make the world the way you want it. Come to terms with your essence, and the rest will slowly follow.

The Spurting of Atum

The Spurting of Atum can be looked at next, and this is a simple enough affair, too. What you must do, at some point, when you pulse alone within the center of Nothingness, is to cry out "Come!" with all your feeling, and with all your strength. You are summoning, stirring, and calling up your own Shadow — your White Shadow as we might term it — who will appear before you in the form of the sex opposite to your own. This form will have all the refinements that the transformation into the opposite sex would make to your own build and features at their *best imagining*.

Within the vast and luminous space, in the heart of that pyramidal castle of primordial forms which, as yet, only contains two forms, you make love to your own Shadow. This is Atum, the Great He/She, mating with his/her own self. It is you, the initiate, coming to terms with your anima or animus.

If you can sustain it, then, after the love-making, imagine yourself as holding hands with your Shadow,

arms spread wide so that you form a great circle
between you both. This is the true Mirror of Hathor into
which every soul has the right to peer on a few occasions
in each incarnation, at certain moments.

Peer in now and see if it vivifies itself. What you
might see are faces — millions and millions of them,
down through the Aeons. What you might see are the
descendants of this essence as they manifest through
time. Which is another way of saying that you, the
present reader, might see your ancestors, leading back
from those within your living memory, back toward the
beginning of your lineage in the First Time.

You, in the form of Atum, have gone back in time to
beget yourself.

At its best, this can be an extremely powerful
experience. At this level, the Mirror of Hathor can show
us extraordinary things. At its worst, it will all end up
as no more than a few fuzzy pictures in your head. But,
in each case, the *effort alone* will produce movement.
This will probably not be perceptible at first. Yet, in
time, the exercise will take each person a very long way
indeed, in more worlds than one.

Shu and Tefnut

There is the stage in which Atum gives birth to Shu
and Tefnut. Once again, the details of this process are
up to the individual who recreates it in magical terms.
Such creative imagination is the vital part of the actual
birth process.

Shu and Tefnut have other names. These can be
researched to advantage, but let us regard them simply
as Air and Moisture — those qualities that made the
land along then Nile habitable, and caused life to grow.
They are also intellect and emotion. We could say about
Shu: "Pure Will, without lust of result, is in every way

perfect," but we must, on Tefnut's behalf, follow this up with: "Love is the law, love under will."

Sometimes it is right for one quality to dominate the other completely within a single person, sometimes it is not right. Whether we should try to bring them into balance or strictly leave the imbalance alone is something that all should answer for themselves. If they cannot, then they are hardly likely to achieve much on any level — much less the magical.

If we decided that such a balance *was* desirable then we could begin to visualize Shu and Tefnut over the months that follow. They have other forms than those given, and these can be found easily enough — or better still you can create your own. Build up scenes in which your emotional life is directly under the sway of Tefnut, while all the intellectual aspects are given to the control of Shu. When you are in full flow emotionally try to spare a brief second to visualize Tefnut. At moments of intellectual exertion raise the image of Shu.

The whole purpose of this is to create links between these two differing qualities and the appropriate images. In time the image of Shu, for example, will automatically alert the subconscious to the fact that a few more brain cells might be needed for the immediate task in hand. In time, when the inner links are made, the image of Shu can suddenly flash into the mind on those occasions when the subconscious knows that more objectivity and analysis are required, as opposed to the emotional reaction otherwise intent on carrying all things before it. It is like having your best friend on hand to make you listen — at those times when you most need to listen.

Can such simple exercises with simple images *really* help expand our intellects and broaden our abilities to feel?

They can if we want them to. It depends on the quality of effort we put in. Quite apart from the obvious benefits of any internal effort, there is also the magical effect of linking with these "God-Forms," for in using this Egyptian scheme, Shu and Tefnut are necessarily our penultimate ancestors. They are also, via that magical technique already given, our very first descendants. They are types and archetypes, to use another terminology. Linking with them is rather like looking into the Mirror of Hathor and asking: "Are there any folk in there with experience of using and abusing extreme intellect? If so, could you gather around this symbol that I am dangling into the mirror and, gradually, make your own experience available to me? Thanks."

Shu and Tefnut, therefore, are more than just obscure cosmological concepts from a world that is now largely lost beneath the sand — they are gathering-points of genetic knowledge.

We can use them if we want.

Nu and Geb

Nu and Geb

We can use their children, Nu and Geb, in a similar manner, although we might profit more by approaching them from a completely different direction.

Nu is the vault of the heavens; Geb is the earth beneath. The atmosphere within is comprised of their parents, Air and Moisture. Without Air and Moisture, the world formed by Nu and Geb would be little different from the (as yet) uninhabitable planet Mars. Visualize Nu and Geb as akin to upper and lower hemispheres in a model cosmos, with Shu and Tefnut the "first swirlings" which make life tenable.

It is in considering Nu and Geb that we can hear the old initiatic lament: "I am a child of Earth, but my race is of the Starry heavens!"

We can, if we want, see within the lion-headed Tefnut one of those hominoid beings of stellar origin who first mated with humankind, producing offspring with earthly (Geb) and stellar (Nu) genes. This would be the true origin of the Sacred Clan, or the Blood Royal. It is also the origin of that dichotomy within us all which makes one part of us live our earthly life to the full, while another part of us is forever striving toward the stars.

Someday humanity will get back there. Not via rocket ships or crude projectile means, or through the intervention of visitors from beyond the galaxy, but by tapping into the nature and consciousness of Geb. The stars will be reached via the Earth Mysteries, and their parallels within the psyche — and particularly via those crystalline structures and substances that excite occultists of all persuasions, without many of them having any clear ideas about the reasons for this enthusiasm.

The Sons of Horus

Imsety
(West)

Qebhsnuf
(East)

Hapi
(North)

Duamutef
(South)

Sons of Horus

We aspire toward Nu, but first we must activate Geb. One of the ways to do this is to study the nature of the Elements, and then work with them. These are the solids, liquids, gases, and radiations which comprise all manifest life, and which are referred to in old alchemical texts as Earth of the Wise, Water of the Wise, Air of the Wise, and Fire of the Wise, respectively. Traditionally they are associated with the four Quarters:

East = Air
South = Fire
West = Water
North = Earth

There are many ways of working with these Elements. Whole books have been written on the topic. For our present scheme, however, we can jump ahead a little and use the Four Sons of Horus to link with each Quarter:

East = Qebhsnuf
South = Duamutef
West = Imsety
North = Hapi

Visualize them strongly and practice regularly. Feel as though you are hovering, burning, floating, or buried. Not in any negative sense, however. You hover and watch and study; you burn with your inner flame and give warmth and illumination; you float upon currents and respond to the ocean depths; you blend with the earth, and life springs up from you.

All of this is very simple, but it is the basis of magic, the pure essence of witchcraft. Build the Elements into your psyche, and Geb, who is the perfection of them all, will come to feel at home.

More of this later.

It is with the children of Nu that we can practice the

"Assumption of the God-Form" technique which is a standard method in most occult systems, in one way or another.

Starting from the Nothingness, in a pure state, visualize yourself in the actual form of a particular God. More than that, *feel* the qualities of the God in question. Intone his name and, while doing so, visualize yourself as growing, larger than human, so that you tower above your world. Great actors do this sort of thing all the time: they can make their presence as large or small as they need. A man, however, should have no real qualms about the Goddess-Form of Isis, for this is not a case of magical transvestism. Rather a man exhibits "Isian" qualities whenever he picks up and soothes his child, while a woman can manifest Osiris when she tongue-lashes wrongdoers. Isis and Osiris, as twins, are energies which exist within us all.

Likewise Set and Nephthys.

Set is dangerous, but he can be extremely useful. We can evoke within ourselves all those petty, trivial, nasty and vindictive faults which blight our lives, and then assume the God-Form of Set with the intention that *he* can have them. This is where they belong, after all. When you actually take on the mantle of Set for this purpose, it is with the specific intention of leaving these particular traits with him. He can then go on to transmute them as appropriate. Or such is the theory. In practice we can get so involved with the dark pleasures of these negative aspects that we can unconsciously end up getting Set to reinforce or even amplify them. Set is useful, but he can be extremely dangerous.

A safer method is to use him in conjunction with Osiris, creating a magical scenario in which Set "devours" your faults. What remains is your own bright

Self which should now be identified with Osiris, and self-wrapped in the luminous swathes of the Osirian mummy-form. These swathes of light are to prevent further infection, to heal, and to seal up the aura. That last purpose is most important of all. We all get "occult infections" from time to time in which pathetic little traits become magnified, almost compulsively, as though we are being egged on by the worst sides of ourselves. They can, with effort, be "set to rights."

Nephthys

With the help of Nephthys, we can become invisible. Not actually, but in a manner of speaking. It was a technique that I used in school at those moments when I least wanted the teacher's attention to fall on me, or for the teacher to ask uncomfortable questions. Green-eyed Nephthys is the one to call upon on such occasions, while imagining yourself as "not there," and seeing, through your teacher's eye, in your place an empty seat and desk. Draw in all your energies as you do this; be very quiet on all levels, like a submarine avoiding sonar.

This is the opposite to being Osiris Risen, or Isis Triumphant. No heads turn when Nephthys enters a crowded room, because she just does not want them to.

All hunters and fishermen know variations on this technique — all learned from the Horned Gods. Hunters must concentrate but not "want" too much. That is the wrong energy to send out, because the quarry can sense such yearning. If the hunter sends out a weak signal of the sort which decodes into "I would rather like to win," then the prey will know, and the hunter will catch or shoot nothing. If instead the signal insists "I cannot fail," then it becomes a different hunt altogether.

Nephthys, the Invisible One, can help us when it comes to hunting all kinds of prey. After all, she managed to capture Osiris easily enough.

Through her we can learn to send out signals — or not — as need be.

Osiris

As happened with Osiris, we can learn to tear ourselves apart into seven portions which relate to instinct, intellect, emotion, and intuition, as well as the states of our lives in the past, present, and future. We must look at positive and negative aspects for each of these portions, so that we have the fourteen pieces that Osiris was split into. We can then create an inner scenario in which these pieces are found, altered for what you hope will be the better, and then joined together again to create a more fulfilled Body of Light. This can be aided with those old medico-astrological diagrams which equate planets and the Zodiac with different parts of the body. This is an attempt to reduce ourselves to our basic, constituent parts and then start again. It can (and should) be used, with a number of the techniques already given.

Anubis

Anubis can be used in his jackal form to guard property, to protect self and belongings, to pace around the magical Circle of Working, and to protect against all kinds of psychic attack. Again, the attitude of the hunter is needed here. When you create this jackal image within your imagination and set it on its appointed task, you have to know that something has been created which is indeed real and true on its own level, and which will perform its job.

Also, it can be extraordinary exercise for magicians to assume the Anubis God-Form, complete with *uas* wand, and then visualizing themselves stepping through that symbol for the *Duat,* the ⬠. Here they are stepping directly into their own subconscious minds. On all occasions, magicians *must* make the return step, and write down whatever they may have seen, or experienced, even if this was no more than a general haze.

The Djed Column

There is a form of magic which utilizes the *djed* column. In this, you visualize yourself stepping into the *djed.* This column represents, among other things, a segment of Osiris' spine. It is necessarily alive with those Serpent Fires which maintain the universe. Use of the column in this way can help us link our own sputtering and fizzing serpent energies with the roaring power behind Osiris himself. Used in this way, the *djed* column can prove itself to be one of the most important techniques of all. Like pieces of a hologram, each small portion of a mystery contains the whole mystery within itself. Enter the *djed,* and you enter the spirit of Egypt itself. Enter the *djed,* and you can also find yourself in possession of a time machine. As you step inside and associate yourself with the tremendous forces within, imagine that the column begins to whirl, with you still inside, faster and faster until it hums like a child's top. Listen to that humming — try to remember it. When it stops, step out and observe. Then step back in and return. Work out a way to make it take you forward, or backward, or beyond time altogether.

The Casket of Osiris

You can identify with Osiris in the great box, as he floats down the Nile, secret of all fertility and its source, the incarnation of hope. Identify with Isis in search, or

Isis as she impregnates herself. You can use the Horus Eye to soar out and look for things, or link with Anubis and all his talents by striving to develop your sense of smell. You can do whatever you want, in your own way. Magic always works, in its own way, at its own time, as long as the correct "exchanges of energy" have been made.

The Second Coming

Whenever students of magic first touch upon a Magical Current they always seem to believe that they are in some way inaugurating something of a Second Coming. Sometimes, getting the lines of light all twisted, they come to believe that they *are* the Second Coming. What they are really doing, however, is inaugurating the Descent of Light into the microcosm of their own psyches.

Those who begin to use the techniques given here, and develop them for their own needs will find Horus emerging from within them. Whatever Ankh-f-n-Khonsu may have done in the larger world, the true Aeon of Horus is ever-becoming within ourselves. All we have to do is find Osiris, the Horned God, and bring him to life again in terms that we can appreciate for ourselves. Use his vital essence to make the spirit of wonder grow within, and try to express that in the outer world. Once that is done, the New Age will start to manifest itself through each individual according to the tone and style of this bright and soaring young God.

These, then, are some deliberately sparse and simple techniques which we can use to go on with. Readers can and must flesh them out and adapt them to taste. If they really want to learn more about working with the Elements, using Magic Mirrors, creating Names of

Power, and all those techniques which have been given in detail in a host of other books, then they will search them out themselves, beginning perhaps with the titles recommended in the final chapter. That searching is itself a part of the magic. If readers are not really interested in such effort, then they will never make it as magicians.

Or, to use a sexual analogy — which is entirely appropriate to any book on the Fertility God — think of these techniques as a type of foreplay which may, if we are skillful, deserving, and just plain lucky, enable us to achieve the greatest kind of Union of them all ...

But now we can forget about Osiris for a while and look at Herne, bearing in mind that it does not pay to mix magical systems.

If we want to find Herne, we must find our own holy places first. Every person must find a hill, valley, stream or river, stone or wood which is sacred to him or her alone. If you have the stability or are at the age so that the place where you now live will also be, in all probability, the place where you will die, then these features should be found in that particular area where you conduct your life. It does not matter whether this is in the heart of a major city or lost within some rural wilderness. We have to reach toward the magical energy within the land.

In this respect every would-be magician must ask him or herself: Why am I *here* — in this specific place upon the Earth? What is the magic within this particular geographical area which has brought me here — for good or ill, richer or poorer, better or worse?

The only certain answer we can offer to this in advance is to assure the individual that the "spirit of place" itself will, in due course, make such reasons abundantly clear to whomever needs to know.

One thing that can be done on intellectual levels to help make the links is to research all that can be found about local myth and history — even of the contemporary sort. The land is a living being with stories to tell. Quite often, like any old person, it craves someone to listen. The language of myth and legend is one of the tongues it can use. Those types of localized hauntings known as "place-memories" are another.

If, however, after much consideration, it is decided that the area in question is certainly not going to be the ultimate place where the person will die, and the individual has no intention whatsoever of trying to work with the area, then other holy places must be chosen, and regular visits made. Or if age or circumstance preclude this, then such visits can be made in the imagination — which is often the truest method of all. They will be no less effective if all the activity is kept within the head and heart. Time and space are relative, after all.

Very often, though, the land itself will seem to exert a will of its own. Magicians will find themselves drawn to a particular place time and again, as circumstances seem to conspire against them. They will find themselves bound to a locality for reasons that will only slowly become apparent, but which have little to do with karma in the human sense and more to do with the Earth-consciousness seeking to work out its own especial destiny via certain individuals.

We should begin with a hill, really. They are good starting points. They are in fact physical parallels of those inner peaks of consciousness which reach toward divinity. All must find their own "holy hill" or "place of power," to use a hackneyed term, without reference to anything or anyone else.

Most young people in Britain, as already mentioned,

regard Glastonbury Tor as the heart-chakra of the world — and perhaps the universe. So it may be, but they limit themselves. Every hill can be made into the heart-chakra of the universe, and there is a marvelous kind of magic to be achieved in doing so with that secret place found by yourself alone.

Let us assume that you have found a hill — or, as is often the case, that a hill has found you. Let us assume that you have found out as much about its history — if there is any — that you can, and you are able to make an actual visit. Before the visit, spend some time mentally dwelling upon the hill's image. Send it a mental message that you are coming, and hope to be well received. On the day in question, when the hill looms before you, it must be approached as you would approach a venerable old man of letters whom you have long admired. That is to say, the attitude should be respectful, but not obsequious; attentive, but not dumb; responsive, but not dramatic. The consciousness inside the hill has not got the slightest interest in what you wear, so you may as well wear ordinary and practical clothing of the most comfortable kind. Robes or nudity are only appropriate for certain individuals. The hill won't care.

When you have climbed as high as is feasible — though preferably to its summit — all you must do is say: "Here I am. My name is_____. I will do no harm to this place. All I want to do is learn." This must be said not so much in words, but in attitude. No assumption should be made that the hill actually wants you there then, or at any other time. In various ways, it will let you know.

This simple but crucial beginning can be combined with an old occult technique which involves the magician sending a tendril of light down from the mid-brain area, down the spinal column, down and into the hill and — ultimately — to the very heart of the Earth. The tip of this tendril should be visualized as spreading itself out, like roots. Visualize this, sustain it, and synchronize the energy-flow with your breathing: breathe out and send your own essence into the hill; breathe in and draw the hill's essence into your psyche. Be watchful of any images that may arise. Make a note of everything, as always,

If the hill has been inhabited in previous eras, then you must at some point very early on make acknowledgements to those who have gone before. It is their place, after all. Be humble, be simple, ask for their help. Insist that you have not come to despoil or betray. Tell them simple things about yourself.

My own holy place (which is not the plateau on which I live) was once a hill-fort at a time when Britain was almost entirely covered by forest. The problem was in finding some link between myself and those who had lived and died upon the steep slopes several thousand years before. Sitting very still, very small, acutely aware of the presences, the ghosts, the words which enabled the link to be made were: "The people who lived here once knew love . . . and so do I." Whether it is love of mother, father, siblings, wife, children, sport, food, laughter, or war, it is the one link between the ages that we can all call upon. Again — and this cannot be said too often — it has nothing to do with mere words upon the lips, but the linking of sympathies.

One other thing we can do, and *must* do, is bring a gift to the hill on each visit. Any gift will do. Coins will do fine. It is not the actual value which is important but the associations in the back of the mind. The coins should be pushed into the earth with some brief and simple ceremony. Food is just as suitable, and this should be left on some prominent rock, as if on an altar.

It does not matter that the food will be eaten by animals or the coins found by children and pocketed. In each case these will represent a gift from the hill to them, with yourself as mediator.

For those who live some distance from the hill, a useful method is to acquire a a good quality chain with a suitably symbolic pendant. Over a few weeks, spend time holding this piece of jewelry while visualizing the hill. Constantly associate the two. This can be done quite easily, in countless different ways.

On the next visit to the actual place, the pendant should then be removed and buried at some focal point. From then on, whenever you are at home and want to "call up" the spirit of the hill, you simply need to wear the chain alone: the rest of it is already there, within the Earth, linked within your psyche for all time.

What is being aimed for, ultimately, is a kind of shamanic identification between the psyche of the magician and the spirit of the land. This is not shamanism as the American Indians understand it, but it is closely related nonetheless. It was expressed in the Arthurian Mysteries as "The King and the Land are One," which was often extended to "The Land and the People are One." We might re-phrase it to read "As without, so within: there is no difference."

Now this type of magic can also be practiced by Christians. But, because of the two-way identification, a Christian must necessarily worship the land as he worships his God. Yet, as already stated, the land today is like a raped woman — raped and badly battered; the *last* thing such a woman wants or needs is worship. As Neo-Pagans committed to working with our gods, we must offer this woman-spirit of the land whatever help and healing she needs. We heal ourselves and we heal her; if we can heal her, we can begin to heal ourselves. As without, so within — there is no difference.

We can use these techniques for the hill with the other natural features as well. They will all respond in their own way. Tracking up the local river, for example, from the mouth to its source, can be done in conjunction with some personal introspection about your own life from the present day (the river mouth), right back through your childhood, your parents' lives, and on and on through your lineage. At the very source, if this sort of charged brooding has been carefully planned, coordinated, and ritualized, you can deliberately call upon the entire circle of your ancestors. Every person has the right to do so once in his or her life and the ancestors have to listen. Pour out whatever angst you have, leave with them whatever bad luck or illness they seem to have passed down to you. They have to listen. On other occasions, you can call them but they no longer have to come. The point is that, on future invocations, they will come out of love and respect and interest, and for those reasons only. So it is a matter of getting yourself straight with them as wisely and decently as you can the first time. Think about and plan this exercise carefully.

All natural features, then, whether they are hills, streams, rivers, lakes, woods, individual rocks, or trees, have an "energy-consciousness" of their own which can make its presence felt, and teach us things. Not quickly, but surely. Many natural features have guardian spirits attached to them — although that is a crude way of putting it. To return briefly to the Egyptian system, there is the story of how Horus could allow Osiris some brief freedom in the upper world by taking his place within the *Tuat*. Likewise, when magicians become identified with power-places of their own finding and (accidentally or otherwise) sink their energies into them, then the inherent spirit of the place may well emerge in classic dragon-form. It is more than an artificial elemental of the sort beloved in psychic battles: it is a creature of the Inner Earth which is part of our oldest selves. What happens then, is entirely a matter between you and it. In Qabalistic terms, this is Malkuth reuniting with Daath (where it came from in the first place), or Earth reuniting with Inner Earth. The priest finds that the Earth herself becomes his priestess, and the relationship is an entirely sensual one. The dragon is child and expression of it all.

At some point during all this, the magician might try to make deliberate contact with Herne or Fiân.

You can lead into this by a simple exercise which involves equating each half of the brain with a particular key-name. The left brain might be EL and the right ELLA; or AB and ABBA, and so on. Do whatever feels best. Normal consciousness, as marked by the ceaseless internal monologue, would be thought of as EL-consciousness. So we must attempt to stimulate the right side of the brain deliberately by intoning EL-LA, EL-LA, EL-LA, and by switching off this monologue entirely, concentrating only on the sound. Do it with your jaw loose but your lips closed — people will only think you are humming as you walk along. But as you walk, and intone, you are a camera, no more. You watch but do not interpret; hear but do not analyze. Later, much later and after much practice, you can learn to activate the right brain by repeatedly intoning "Herna," in the same way. This is coupled with an Assumption of the God-Form, and an attempt to view the countryside around as a stag would see it, in terms of grazing, shelter, and sanctuary.

Exactly the same methods can be used whether the

person favors the cerebrum/cerebellum alternatives in analyzing and altering consciousness. It is intent which is everything.

Now you can also begin to create your "inner glade," which will be a secure place within your consciousness where you can go to commune with your God.

Visualize a grove of trees across a broad, upward-sloping field, You enter this field through a particular gate and find yourself walking up to the grove by a well-worn though narrow trail. It leads you between huge, ancient, and broad-leaved oaks, into a clearing that is bright with the light of the Moon. There are two tall, jagged standing stones there; one of them represents Life, and the other Death. They are as far apart as your outstretched arms and as tall as you can reach. They thrill you with energy. Here, before the stones, you stand naked and call upon your Horned God — the supreme expression of your most secret self. Here within the glade, within your own psyche, he will come and meet you.

The very first time this exercise is performed is often the most dramatic, for novelty has its own value even in the world of magic. Most other times, the picture that forms before your inner eye will be a flat projection and nothing more. No matter how hard you try, and no matter how carefully you do not try, the picture will refuse to take on depth. That is perfectly normal. Similar things happen in the outer world every day. But the Horned God comes when he wants and you need, and there will be moments when this magical glade will take form of its own accord. You will feel it happen, feel a peculiar agitation in the right side of the brain. When you sit down to make contact, the glade will take on a curious sparkle; you will know beyond any doubt that you are, in some strange way, in Another Place.

As always, keep it simple when you talk to Herne. He and the rest of the Horned Gods are not interested in long harangues or whining self-pity. If you have to ask him for anything remember that, while he gives, he also takes away. This is all part of the Law of Exchange, which he will teach you himself, if you ask him.

If any visions arise, then make a note of them; but never let them carry you away. The mind can do some extraordinary tricks. Visions are not always to be trusted. Watch, listen, feel, make notes of it all. Occasionally demand that our Gods show us what they are made of. At intervals, when it seems appropriate, challenge them. If they will not or cannot respond by means of "signs following," then they are not worth worrying about.

There are many traps, many pitfalls, and even more pratfalls to be made in this direction, but it is all part of the learning process. In all cases, be like Herne yourself: strike bold postures when you think it necessary, and always travel light.

What will happen is that your "own" people will gradually drift into your orbit as if by accident. People with whom you are bound on inner levels will come to add teachings and experiences of their own. Sagas of what seem to be group reincarnation tend to activate themselves at these times, although reincarnation in the orthodox sense is by no means as universal as is assumed: not everyone reincarnates. It all depends upon whether they have the *spark,* and having the spark has nothing to do with being good or virtuous. Sometimes, it is not so much a question of us having *previous* lives as having *other* lives. Herne or Fiân will explain that too, if you ask them. Even so, your own life will become filled with synchronistic events to such an extent that they will seem commonplace, utterly natural and scarcely worthy of comment.

Invoke Herne, and you set yourself the highest of challenges. Attempt to wear his helm, and you aim for the majesty of Kings, no less. Long climbs and many rapid falls — that is the nature of life, that is the spirit of Herne. You have to ask yourself if you dare, and if it will all be worth it in the end . . .

Which, in essence, is all there is to it. The Horned God from humanity's dawn awakened within the psyche by a few simple exercises vitalized by a desire for — what? Power? Love? Wisdom? Perhaps desire alone is sufficient, regardless of what the Buddha said.

In fact, if the reader has got this far with any degree of excitement, challenge, or interest whatsoever, the initial work will already have begun. The eyelids of the sleeping God will have begun to flicker in that rapid eye movement which signifies dreaming. So what is he dreaming? He is dreaming you into awareness, into a New Age. When his eyes open, so will yours.

The Horned God described in this book is a lean and hungry creature as he stands now, who has gone many centuries without much nourishment. Fill him up now — with your own wonder and delight, to feast with, or on, when the moment comes. That is what Horned Gods are for, after all. I have shown him to you in the form of the stag, ram, and bull, and would only point out in respect to the latter that where there are bulls, there might also be bullshit.

Have I added any? Perhaps, perhaps not. I will only promise that, if I have done so, it will have been placed with great skill, and with the full knowledge that bullshit is in itself a wondrously potent fertilizer.

The path of the most ancient God is now stretching before you, already glistening in your spirit if you but knew it. Enjoy the journey — but watch your step!

Further Reading

Those interested in the development of the Horned God's worship in this century can do no better than read the books of Doreen Valiente, who is one of the most lucid and judicious writers on this particular topic. Especially recommended are *The ABC of Witchcraft* and *Witchcraft for Tomorrow*. From the historical viewpoint, Margaret Murray's *The God of the Witches* and *The Divine King in England* are the two standard works — both of which have been given an admirable kind of synthesis and development in Michael Harrison's *The Roots of Witchcraft*. Between them, these writers have analyzed and presented the available material so well that they have made it exceedingly difficult for any newcomers to say anything radically different!

As far as Egypt goes, Veronica Ions gives a nice introduction and guided tour through the complex minefield of "Symbolist" analysis in her *Egyptian Mythology*. Arthur Versluis has achieved a certain cache in this field with his *Egyptian Mysteries*, but R.T. Rundle Clark, in his little-trumpeted *Myth and Symbol in Ancient Egypt*, shows both a greater substance and a scholarly awareness of mythologies which are more purely Western. From the more esoteric side, the essays on Egypt by C. R. F. Seymour in *The Forgotten Mage* (edited by Dolores Ashcroft-Nowicki) shows the insight of a man who really had been a priest in that country — and a damned good one. Murry Hope's *Practical Egyptian Magic* gives enough clear and effective techniques to enable anyone to build his or her own Egyptian temple on inner and outer levels.

From the Arthurian point of view, the books of Geoffrey Ashe cover all the more exoteric aspects of that topic, while Gareth Knight's *The Secret Traditions in Arthurian Legend* takes us on a wondrous journey into the depths. The Mysteries of Avalon generally have been more than adequately dealt with by Christine Hartley in her *The Western Mystery Tradition,* although this has largely been superseded by John and Caitlin Matthews' *The Western Way,* which goes some way toward recreating a Tradition that was once feared completely lost.

Into those realms which are less easy to classify are the books of Kenneth Grant, notably *Aleister Crowley and the Hidden God.* Grant is one of the few truly original (and highly controversial) writers and practitioners of magic today. R. J. Stewart's *The Underworld Initiation* can take us on an extraordinary inner journey despite his rather labored style, while Dolores Ashcroft-Nowicki's *The Shining Paths* must surely be the standard book on that technique known as pathworking. It is difficult to see how anyone can do this sort of thing better In the same direction, her *Ritual Magic Workbook* will fill in those practical details so conspicuously lacking in my own final chapter. Finally, there are the books by William G. Gray, notably the Sangreal Series, and *Megalithic Magic,* whose themes have constantly merged and re-emerged among those that I sometimes try to fancy are peculiarly my own.

STAY IN TOUCH

On the following pages you will find listed, with their current prices, some of the books now available on related subjects. Your book dealer stocks most of these, and will stock new titles in the Llewellyn series as they become available. We urge your patronage.

However, to obtain our full catalog, to keep informed of new titles as they are released and to benefit from informative articles and helpful news, you are invited to write for our bi-monthly news magazine/catalog. A sample copy is free, and it will continue coming to you at no cost as long as you are an active mail customer. Or you may keep it coming for a full year with a donation of just $5.00 in U.S.A. & Canada ($20.00 overseas, first class mail). Many bookstores also have *The Llewellyn New Times* available to their customers. Ask for it.

Stay in touch! In *The Llewellyn New Times'* pages you will find news and reviews of new books, tapes and services, announcements of meetings and seminars, articles helpful to our readers, news of authors, advertising of products and services, special money-making opportunities, and much more.

The Llewellyn New Times
P.O. Box 64383-Dept. 672, St. Paul, MN 55164-0383, U.S.A.
• • •

TO ORDER BOOKS AND TAPES

If your book dealer does not have the books described on the following pages readily available, you may order them direct from the publisher by sending full price in U.S. funds, plus $1.50 for postage and handling for orders *under* $10.00; $3.00 for orders *over* $10.00. There are no postage and handling charges for orders over $50. UPS Delivery: We ship UPS whenever possible. Delivery guaranteed. Provide your street address as UPS does not deliver to P.O. Boxes. UPS to Canada requires a $50 minimum order. Allow 4–6 weeks for delivery. Orders outside the U.S.A. and Canada: Airmail—add retail price of book; add $5 for each non-book item (tapes, etc.); add $1 per item for surface mail.

FOR GROUP STUDY AND PURCHASE

Because there is a great deal of interest in group discussion and study of the subject matter of this book, we feel that we should encourage the adoption and use of this particular book by such groups by offering a special "quantity" price to group leaders or "agents."

Our Special Quantity Price for a minimum order of five copies of *Earth God Rising* is $32.85 cash-with-order. This price includes postage and handling within the United States. Minnesota residents must add 6.5% sales tax. For additional quantities, please order in multiples of five. For Canadian and foreign orders, add postage and handling charges as above. Credit card (VISA, Master Card, American Express) orders are accepted. Charge card orders only may be phoned free ($15.00 minimum order) within the U.S.A. or Canada by dialing 1-800-THE-MOON. Customer service calls dial 1-612-291-1970. Mail Orders to:

LLEWELLYN PUBLICATIONS
P.O. Box 64383-Dept. 672 / St. Paul, MN 55164-0383, U.S.A.

ANCIENT MAGICKS FOR A NEW AGE
by Alan Richardson and Geoff Hughes

With two sets of personal magickal diaries, this book details the work of magicians from two different eras. In it, you can learn what a particular magician is experiencing in this day and age, how to follow a similar path of your own, and discover correlations to the workings of traditional adepti from almost half a century ago.

The first set of diaries are from Christine Hartley and show the magick performed within the Merlin Temple of the Stella Matutina, an offshoot of the Hermetic Order of the Golden Dawn, in the years 1940-42. The second set are from Geoff Hughes, and detail his magickal work during 1984-86. Although he was not at that time a member of any formal group, the magick he practiced was under the same aegis as Hartley's. The third section of this book, written by Hughes, shows how you can become your own Priest or Priestess and make contact with Merlin.

The magick of Christine Hartley and Geoff Hughes are like the poles of some hidden battery that lies beneath the Earth and beneath the years. There is a current flowing between them, and the energy is there for you to tap.

0-87542-671-9, 320 pgs., illus., 6 × 9 $12.95

LEAVES OF YGGDRASIL
by Freya Aswynn

Leaves of Yggdrasil is the first book to offer an extensive presentation of Rune concepts, mythology and magical applications inspired by Dutch/Frisian traditional lore.

Author Freya Aswynn, although writing from a historical perspective, offers her own interpretations of this data based on her personal experience with the system. Freya's inborn, native gift of psychism enables her to work as a runic seeress and consultant in depth-psychological rune readings, one of which is detailed in a chapter on *Runic Divination*.

Leaves of Yggdrasil emphasizes the feminine mysteries and the function of the Northern priestesses. It unveils a complete and personal system of the rune magic that will fascinate students of mythology, spirituality, psychism and Teutonic history, for this is not only a religious autobiography but also a historical account of the ancient Northern European culture.

0-87542-024-9, 5 1/4 x 8, 304 pgs. $12.95

COMING INTO THE LIGHT
by Gerald Schueler

COMING INTO THE LIGHT is the name that the ancient Egyptians gave to a series of magickal texts known to us today as The Book of the Dead. Coming into the Light provides modern translations of these famous texts, and shows that they are not simply religious prayers or spells to be spoken over the body of a dead king, but rituals to be performed by living magicians who seek to know the truth about themselves and their world.

Basic Egyptian philosophical and religious concepts are explained and explored, and ritual texts for a wide variety of magickal use are presented. For example, the Ritual of the Opening of the Mouth, perhaps the most well-known of Egyptian rituals, allows a magician to enter into the higher regions of the Magickal Universe without losing consciousness. Enough of this ancient wisdom has been passed down to us so that today we may gain a unique insight into the workings of those powerful magicians who performed their operations thousands of years ago.

0-87542-713-8, 384 pgs., 6 x 9, color plates, softcover $14.95

MAGICAL RITES FROM THE CRYSTAL WELL
by Ed Fitch

In nature, and in the Earth, we look and find beauty. Within ourselves we find a well from which we may draw truth and knowledge. And when we draw from this well, we rediscover that we are all children of the Earth.

The simple rites in this book are presented to you as a means of finding your own way back to nature; for discovering and experiencing the beauty and the magic of unity with the source.

These are the celebrations of the seasons: at the same time they are rites by which we attune ourselves to the flow of the force—the energy of life. These are rites of passage by which we celebrate the major transitions we all experience in life.

Here are the Old Ways, but they are also the Ways for Today.

0-87542-230-6, 147 pages, 7 x 10, illus., softcover. $9.95

THE LLEWELLYN ANNUALS

Llewellyn's MOON SIGN BOOK: Approximately 400 pages of valuable information on gardening, fishing, weather, stock market forecasts, personal horoscopes, good planting dates, and general instructions for finding the best date to do just about anything! Articles by prominent forecasters and writers in the fields of gardening, astrology, politics, economics and cycles. This special almanac, different from any other, has been published annually since 1906. It's fun, informative and has been a great help to millions in their daily planning.   **State year $4.95**

Llewellyn's SUN SIGN BOOK: Your personal horoscope for the entire year! All 12 signs are included in one handy book. Also included are forecasts, special feature articles, and an action guide for each sign. Monthly horoscopes are written by Gloria Star, author of *Optimum Child*, for your personal Sun Sign. Articles on a variety of subjects written by well-known astrologers from around the country. Much more than just a horoscope guide! Entertaining and fun the year round.

State year $4.95

Llewellyn's DAILY PLANETARY GUIDE and ASTROLOGER'S DATE-BOOK: Includes all of the major daily aspects plus their exact times in Eastern and Pacific time zones, lunar phases, signs and voids plus their times, planetary motion, a monthly ephemeris, sunrise and sunset tables, special articles on the planets, signs, aspects, a business guide, planetary hours, rulerships, and much more. Large 5¼ × 8 format for more writing space, spiral bound to lay flat, address and phone listings, time zone conversion chart and blank horoscope chart.   **State year $6.95**

Llewellyn's MAGICKAL ALMANAC
Edited by Ray Buckland
The Magickal Almanac examines some of the many forms that Magick can take, allowing the reader a peek behind a veil of secrecy into Egyptian, Shamanic, Wiccan and other traditions. The almanac pages for each month provide information important in the many aspects of working Magick: sunrise and sunset, phases and signs of the Moon, and festival dates, as well as the tarot card, herb, incense, color, and ingresses of the Sun and Moon associated with the particular day.

Articles addressing one form of Magick, with rituals the reader can easily follow, appear each month. An indispensable guide for all interested in the Magickal arts, *The Magickal Almanac* features writing by some of the most prominent authors in the field.

State year $9.95

EARTH POWER:
TECHNIQUES OF NATURAL MAGIC
by Scott Cunningham
Magick is the art of working with the forces of Nature to bring about necessary, and desired, changes. The forces of Nature—expressed through Earth, Air, Fire and Water—are our "spiritual ancestors" who paved the way for our emergence from the pre-historic seas of creation. Attuning to, and working with these energies in magick not only lends you the power to affect changes in your life, it also allows you to sense your own place in the larger scheme of Nature. Using the "Old Ways" enables you to live a better life, and to deepen your understanding of the world about you. The tools and powers of magick are around you, waiting to be grasped and utilized. This book gives you the means to put Magick into your life, shows you how to make and use the tools, and gives you spells for every purpose.
0-87542-121-0, 176 pgs., 51/4 x 8, illus., softcover $8.95

WICCA: A GUIDE FOR THE SOLITARY PRACTITIONER
by Scott Cunningham
Wicca is a book of life, and how to live magically, spiritually, and wholly attuned with Nature. It is a book of sense and common sense, not only about Magick, but about religion and one of the most critical issues of today: how to achieve the much needed and wholesome relationship with out Earth. Cunningham presents Wicca as it is today—a gentle, Earth-oriented religion dedicated to the Goddess and God. This book fulfills a need for a practical guide to solitary Wicca—a need which no previous book has fulfilled.

Here is a positive, practical introduction to the religion of Wicca, designed so that any interested person can learn to practice the religion alone, anywhere in the world. It presents Wicca honestly and clearly, without the pseudo-history that permeates other books. It shows that Wicca is a vital, satisfying part of twentieth century life.

This book presents the theory and practice of Wicca from an individual's perspective. The section on the Standing Stones Book of Shadows contains solitary rituals for the Esbats and Sabbats. This book, based on the author's nearly two decades of Wiccan practice, presents an eclectic picture of various aspects of this religion. Exercises designed to develop magical proficiency, a self-dedication ritual, herb, crystal and rune magic, recipes for Sabbat feasts, are included in this excellent book.
0-87542-118-0, 240 pgs., 6 x 9, illus., softcover $9.95

CELTIC MAGIC
by D. J. Conway

Many people, not all of Irish descent, have a great interest in the ancient Celts and the Celtic pantheon, and *Celtic Magic* is the map they need for exploring this ancient and fascinating magical culture.

Celtic Magic is for the reader who is either a beginner or intermediate in the field of magic, providing an extensive "how-to" of practical spell-working. There are many books on the market dealing with the Celts and their beliefs, but none guide the reader to a practical application of magical knowledge for use in everyday life. There is also an in-depth discussion of Celtic deities and the Celtic way of life and worship, so that an intermediate practitioner can expand upon the spellwork to build a series of magical rituals.

Presented in an easy-to-understand format, *Celtic Magic* is for anyone Searching for new spells that can be worked immediately, without elaborate or rare materials, and with minimal time and preparation.

0-87542-136-9, 240 pgs., mass market, illus.   **$3.95**

WHEEL OF THE YEAR: Living the Magickal Life
by Pauline Campanelli

If like most Pagans you feel elated from the celebrations of the Sabbats and hunger for that feeling during the long weeks between Sabbats, then *Wheel of the Year* can help you to put the joy of celebration and the fulfillment of magic into your everyday life.

The wealth of seasonal rituals and charms contained in *Wheel of the Year* are all easily performed with materials readily available, and are simple and concise enough that the practitioner can easily adapt them to work within the framework of his or her Pagan tradition. Learn how to perform fire magic in November, the best time to make magic wand and why, the ancient magical secrets of objects found on a beach, and the secret Pagan symbolism of Christmas tree ornaments.

Whether you are a newcomer to the Craft or found your way back many years ago, *Wheel of the Year* will be an invaluable reference book in your practical magical library. It is filled with magic and ritual for everyday life and will enhance any system of Pagan Ritual.

0-87542-091-5, 192 pp., 7 × 10, illustrated   **$9.95**

BIRTH OF A MODERN SHAMAN
by Cynthia Bend and Tayja Wiger

This is the amazing true story of Tayja Wiger. As a child she had been beaten and sexually abused. As an adult she was beaten and became a prostitute. To further her difficulties she was a member of a minority, a Native American Sioux, and was also legally blind.

Tayja's courage and will determined that she needed to make changes in her life. This book follows her physical and emotional healing through the use of Transactional Analysis and Re-Birthing, culminating in the healing of her blindness by the Spiritualistic Minister Marilyn Rossner, through the laying-on-of-hands.

Astrology and graphology are used to show the changes in Tayja as her multiple personalities, another problem from which she suffered, were finally integrated into one. Tayja has become both a shaman and a healer.

In *Birth of a Modern Shaman* there are powerful skills anyone can develop by becoming a shaman, the least of which is becoming balanced, at peace with the world around you, productive and happy. By using the techniques in this book you will move toward a magickal understanding of the universe that can help you achieve whatever you desire, and can help *you* to become a modern shaman.

0-87542-034-6, 272 pgs., 6 x 9, illus., softcover   **$9.95**

IN THE SHADOW OF THE SHAMAN
by Amber Wolfe

Presented in what the author calls a "cookbook shamanism" style, this book shares recipes, ingredients, and methods of preparation for experiencing some very ancient wisdoms—wisdoms of Native American and Wiccan traditions, as well as contributions from other philosophies of Nature, as they are used in the shamanic way. Wolfe encourages us to feel confident and free to use her methods to cook up something new, completely on our own. This blending of ancient formulas and personal methods represents what Ms. Wolfe calls *Aquarian Shamanism*.

Along with increased interest in shamanic ways—the deep, direct ways of Nature—there have also come many people who urge us to follow a certain set method to attune to shamanic energies. In this book you are encouraged to be ever mindful of your truest teacher, the guide within. Wolfe encourages you to follow that wisdom that dwells within your center. When you do this, you are following the heart of the shamanic path; and this makes us open to the wonderful, pure energies of Nature.

In the Shadow of the Shaman is designed to communicate in the most practical, direct ways possible, so that the wisdom and the energy may be shared for the benefit of all. Whatever your system or tradition, you will find this to be a valuable book, a resource, a friend, a gentle guide and support on your journey. Dancing in the shadow of the shaman, you will find new dimensions of Spirit.

0-87542-888-6, 384 pgs., 6 x 9, illus., softcover   **$12.95**

THE RITES OF ODIN
by Ed Fitch

The ancient Northern Europeans knew a rough magic drawn from the grandeur of vast mountains and deep forests, of rolling oceans and thundering storms. Their rites and beliefs sustained the Vikings, accompanying them to the New World and to the steppes of Central Asia. Now, for the first time, this magic system is brought compellingly into the present by author Ed Fitch.

This is a complete source volume on Odinism. It stresses the ancient values as well as the magic and myth of this way of life. The author researched his material in Scandinavia and Germany, and drew from anthropological and historical sources in Eastern and Central Europe.

A full cycle of ritual is provided, with rites of passage, magical spells, divination techniques, and three sets of seasonal rituals: solitary, group and family. *The Rites of Odin* also contains extensive "how-to" sections on planning and conducting Odinist ceremonies, including preparation of ceremonial implements and the setting up of ritual areas. Each section is designed to stand alone for easier reading and for quick reference. A bibliography is provided for those who wish to pursue the historical and anthropological roots of Odinism further.

0-87542-224-1, 384 pgs., 6 X 9 $12.95

EVOKING THE PRIMAL GODDESS
by William G. Gray

In our continuing struggle to attain a higher level of spiritual awareness, one thing has become clear: we need to cultivate and restore the matriarchal principle to its proper and equal place in our conceptions of Deity. Human history and destiny are determined by our Deity concepts, whatever they may be, and for too long the results of a predominantly masculine God in war, brutality and violence have been obvious.

In *Evoking the Primal Goddess*, renowned occultist William G. Gray takes you on a fascinating, insightful journey into the history and significance of the Goddess in religion. For the first time anywhere, he shows that the search for the Holy Grail was actually a movement within the Christian church to bring back the feminine element into the concept of Deity. He also shows how you can evoke your own personal image of the Mother ideal through practical rituals and prayer.

It has been said that whatever happens in spiritual levels of life will manifest itself on physical ones as well. By following Gray's techniques, you can re-balance both your male and your female polarities into a single spiritual individuality of practical Power!

0-87542-271-3, 5¼ x 8, 192 pgs. $9.95